"Dennis, we're just not suited to one another," Roxy insisted.

"What do you mean?" he asked.

"I fly off the handle, I'm too committed to my work, and I jump out of airplanes—"

His hands swept up her spine, then pulled her close to him. "What about need? Need between a man and a woman. Yours and mine." He drew her even closer. "Kiss me, Roxy. Prove you're right."

"Well, I do want to kiss you for helping Maggie get a job," she said, and leaned close.

He gave her the lightest of kisses. She barely felt it as he kept the contact coolly impersonal. "Why must you give yourself an excuse when you kiss me?" He brushed her jaw with his knuckles. "You push people away so you don't have to take risks."

"What are you talking about?" she demanded.

"This." Her breath quickened as he tucked her between his muscular legs. "I dare you to kiss me the way you're dying to. With no excuses."

"That's not fair, Dennis."

"You're petrified you might feel too much."

"No!"

"Prove it. I dare you to let your feelings go . . . ."

## WHAT ARE *LOVESWEPT* ROMANCES?

They are stories of true romance and touching emotion. We believe those two very important ingredients are constants in our highly sensual and very believable stories in the *LOVESWEPT* line. Our goal is to give you, the reader, stories of consistently high quality that may sometimes make you laugh, sometimes make you cry, but are always fresh and creative and contain many delightful surprises within their pages.

Most romance fans read an enormous number of books. Those they truly love, they keep. Others may be traded with friends and soon forgotten. We hope that each *LOVESWEPT* romance will be a treasure—a "keeper." We will always try to publish

*LOVE STORIES YOU'LL NEVER FORGET*
*BY AUTHORS YOU'LL ALWAYS REMEMBER*

The Editors

**Doris Parmett**
**Fiery Angel**

BANTAM BOOKS
NEW YORK · TORONTO · LONDON · SYDNEY · AUCKLAND

FIERY ANGEL
A Bantam Book / August 1992

If you would be interested in receiving protective vinyl
covers for your Loveswept books, please write to this address
for information:

Loveswept
Bantam Books
P.O. Box 985
Hicksville, NY 11802

ISBN 0-553-44296-1

Published simultaneously in the United States and Canada

# *One*

---

The blue Cessna leveled off at ten thousand feet. Roxy Harris, suited up in an F-111 parachute, waited for the signal from her jumpmaster, Bob Arnouth.

He tapped her shoulder, then shouted above the roar of the plane's engines. "Remember to check your altimeter speed and pull the rip cord at three thousand feet. Have a good ride. Go!"

She stepped outward, reveling in the sensation of tumbling in space, a brightly plumed bird in yellow coveralls, with a white helmet. Arms and legs spread wide, and with no cloud cover to obscure her vision, she rotated her body to see the vistas below. Rooftops, church steeples, buildings, homes, and cars grew larger as she flew downward. The September sun shone on fields of corn, casting golden highlights on the fertile land.

Skydiving was the supreme high. Only another flyer could understand the thrill. Her mother wished she'd be more sensible. "You love flying, fine," she'd say. "Get married and take a commercial airliner on your honeymoon."

Laughing joyously, Roxy shouted her love of skydiving, her voice trailing behind her. Relying on herself alone, she was free, mistress of the sky, catching rivers of air and riding their currents. She cleared her mind of everything, leaving her worries on the ground. The noiseless air caressed her face, brushed her clothes. Of all the parts of a jump, the electrifying free-fall ranked as her favorite. She had trust in her equipment, trust in her training. Trust in herself.

At three thousand feet she yanked the rip cord and counted, smiling. She was confident, thanks to the training program she had undergone before Bob certified her solo jump. In three seconds a 220-square-foot canopy of red-and-white nylon unfurled, tugging her gently to an upright position.

Suddenly, a burst of wind slammed into the parachute, collapsing the canopy and whipping her jumpsuit to her body. Her heart leaped into her throat as she plummeted out of control. She'd flown into a pilot's and skydiver's nightmare. *Wind shear!* A sudden downdraft of fierce winds rendered her helpless, distorting and squeezing the air from her parachute. Defenseless without the canopy, she plunged earthward. Her only hope, her only chance for life, was to pray she had enough altitude to fly through it and somehow catch a lifesaving current of air. If not, she would die.

Tasting fear, she placed herself in God's hands. Ironically, her life wasn't flashing before her eyes. She was too scared.

"Please, God, I'm not ready."

Clinging desperately to the rigging, a pointed arrow pitching toward certain death, she gulped air into her lungs. Prayerful, she braced herself against the inevitable. Then, at one thousand feet, the maddening descent ended as suddenly as it had begun. In that golden moment her parachute billowed upward. Salty tears fogged her goggles.

"Thank you, Lord."

The terrifying moments had blown her far from her landing site, taking her to an unused section of the airfield. A line of trees, their branches sculpting upward, bordered one side. Once again she gave thanks. She would not crash ignominiously into a tree, nor was she concerned about the rocks that she knew lay in the warm brown earth, where gentle winds ruffled patches of grass. She had walked the entire field, home to foraging rabbits and occasional deer, as part of her training, acquainting herself with the surface of the land in case she was blown off course.

"What the . . . ?"

As she scanned the field, an amazing sight appeared. She could hardly believe her eyes. A man, his arms outstretched, his hands cupped as if ready to catch a ball, zigged and zagged across the field, heading toward her. She glanced around. She was the only chutist in the sky. Oh, no! He had witnessed her harrowing ride and must think she was in trouble. If she landed on him, she'd squash him like an ant. Not to say what she'd do to herself.

Racing from the opposite end of the field, his sweaty palms drying in the air, Dennis Jorden ran as if jet-propelled. His heart beat double-time. The sum total of his knowledge of parachuting came from watching old war movies, yet he knew without a doubt the chutist was in dire trouble. He didn't need to be a professional jumper to realize the girl desperately hanging onto her lines could die without his help.

Personally, he avoided heights. In hotels he refused to stay in rooms above the third floor. Why he'd ever decided to go to his first live parachute show he'd never know, but come he had, as if the will to choose had been taken from him, depositing him at Alexandria Field. He glanced around the deserted section of the field, hoping to see others joining in the rescue. Nobody. Not even a chicken or a rabbit. All he saw were stunted grasses and scattered rocks.

"You're it, buddy," he muttered, wishing for a magic genie to make Hulk Hogan or Arnold Schwarzenegger materialize out of thin air to help him catch the chutist.

He changed course slightly to sprint out of the sun's blinding rays. She was coming down fast, kicking her feet, sending him a frantic message to help her.

He powered down, picking up more speed until he neared her projected landing site. His brain whirled. He knew how to give the Heimlich maneuver. He knew how to administer mouth-to-mouth resuscitation. He did not know how to catch a woman crashing down out of the sky. Not without doing major damage to parts of his anatomy, at least. Forget it, he said to himself. He should concentrate on the little he knew of administering first aid.

*Elevate the legs above the heart to stop the blood flow.*

*Keep the victim calm.*

*Get help.*

Thank goodness for his Boy Scout first aid training manual and a few medical segments he'd watched on television. He shouted out to her she'd be okay. Concerned the wind would drown out his voice, he waved his arms. He didn't trust the chute that had finally opened. And judging from her beckoning actions, she didn't either. Calm, he told himself, calm. First and foremost, keep her calm.

Above him, Roxy was anything but serene. She was a riot of terrified nerves; her heartbeat zoomed into the stratosphere.

"I'm not ready for this," she wailed. She had to be able to land and run, or to roll over to take the pressure off her legs. She had to land clear. Nowhere in her training did it say to run smack into a solid wall of man!

Feverishly, she kicked her legs again, hoping the action would alert him to the danger and shoo him away. It didn't. He kept coming.

Looping her arms around the parachute cord, she frantically batted her hands in a final attempt to ward him off. She failed. He stood his ground, growing larger by the second. Panic grabbed her. If she landed on him with the velocity and force of her falling speed, she could kill him or herself.

For nothing!

The coroner would sign her death certificate: death by a well-meaning, brainless idiot!

Fury ripped through her. The Man Upstairs had let her taste the glory of life. Even if she survived this landing, she was going to crack her bones, probably every one of them, thanks to her misguided champion. Instead of helping people, she would become a burden on her parents, who wanted only to see her happily married!

A deep masculine voice raced up to her. "I've got you. Don't worry about me, angel. You're safe. I saw everything. I'll save you."

"Get out of the way or we'll both land in the hospital!" she screamed. For once she wished the law of gravity could be suspended.

"Don't concern yourself about me. I'll save you."

"Deliver me." She hoped to at least keep her teeth after the impact. At the last second she gave her lines a mighty tug and twisted hard.

"Move!" she shouted. Trying to land and run without crashing into him, she missed him by inches but lost her balance. She fell, and her chute pulled her across the ground.

"Ouch! Ouch! Ouch!" she yelped, her rear end finding rocks.

She ground to a bouncing stop, and the air gusted out of her lungs. Her arms felt as if they had been yanked from their sockets. Her teeth rattled. She probed her gums with her tongue. It seemed all her teeth were still connected. Relieved that she was still all intact, she snatched off her goggles and helmet and glared at the man responsible for her near-death collision.

It took Dennis Jorden two seconds to bless fate for directing him to the airfield. Even the ripped coveralls couldn't hide the woman's shapely figure. When she removed her helmet, she freed a tantalizing shower of fiery red hair that settled like glowing embers around her slim shoulders. Vivid green eyes, framed by surprisingly dark lashes, opened wide with fury. He was struck by the deep fire of her luxuriant hair, the compelling green of her eyes. She surpassed pretty. A man would have to be blind to disregard such blessed fortune. He felt unexpectedly happy, and the broad smile on his face reflected his pleasure.

"Welcome to earth, lovely lady. I think we should thank fate for bringing us together."

Roxy shook her head. What do you say to a nut?

She was sure she'd heard him say they should be thanking fate. Cursing might be more like it. While she waited for her breathing to return to normal, she let her gaze travel upward, past a pair of long, sturdy legs encased in jeans. If she were a person who believed in fate—and she wasn't!— she'd have to admit this Viking god with the trim athletic body, the muscular chest that hinted at coiled strength, looked better than any man she'd seen in a long time. Sunlight spilled on his hair, creating a golden nimbus. His features were finely drawn, as if an artist had used a golden paint-brush to accent and highlight. When he crouched down beside her, she noticed his lashes were tipped with dark brown, and his hair was threaded with strokes of molten honey.

Was it possible her frightening fall through the sky had resulted in temporary hallucination? She squeezed her eyes shut, then slowly opened them again. No, he was still there, filling her vision. She had to admit he filled it very well. He gazed at her with gray eyes, defined by the longest lashes she'd ever seen on a man.

"I'm delighted you made it safely," he said.

"Me too." The harness attached to her back made it difficult for her to sit up, and she toppled backward. Immediately a steadying hand supported her. "Don't bother," she muttered, extricating a pointy rock stabbing her buttock.

"You had quite a scare. You're lucky I was here to save you."

Save her! If she'd ripped her chute, her inglorious landing could cost her a fortune. Which she didn't have. She'd loaned her backup chute to a friend to take on a parachuting vacation in Europe. Clarisse would be gone for over a month.

"Did you rip my chute?" she asked.

"I'm concerned about you, not a patch of silk. How do you feel?"

Roxy massaged her aching palms and stinging wrists. "I'm fine. You saw the chute open. What possessed you to interrupt my landing? You could have seriously injured both of us. What about my chute? Did you ruin it?"

Dennis swept his gaze over her. Despite her ungrateful attitude, he hesitated. Although she appeared okay, appearances often were misleading. *Keep the patient calm.*

"Please," she said.

Her desperate tone sent him on a cursory inspection of the chute. He was back in moments. "One long rip, that's all."

"That's all!" she howled. Her shoulders slumped, and the breath shuddered out of her. With one finger she traced the rip on one knee of her coveralls. "Mister, I hope you're satisfied. You just cost me a lot of money."

He glanced over at the colorful chute. "I didn't mean to. How much does one of these things cost?"

"Twenty-five hundred dollars, including a back-up chute. My suit is another hundred-fifty dollars. What else could possibly happen to me?" she said woefully.

He hunkered down, taking the task of massaging her wrists upon himself. "Cheer up," he said. "I didn't plan to be here today, yet here I am. Do you believe in fate?"

"Absolutely not."

"I do," he said with deep conviction. "We were fated to meet this way.

She stared at him in utter disbelief. He really was twisting her near-death experience into an act of fate. She had barreled to earth to land at a crazy man's feet. Why? What could she have possibly done to deserve it?

"If you think almost getting whacked on the jaw with two booted feet is ordained by fate, you're nuts." Provoked beyond endurance, she scowled at him. "I don't believe in fate. Go away."

He stayed put. "I can't. Suppose you need me? You say you're okay, but you could have a concussion."

She rubbed her rump. "On this end? I doubt it."

He cocked his head to one side, admired her tush, then swung his gaze back to her face. "I'm not leaving you. I would never forgive myself."

She heard the finality in his voice, saw it in his expression. He had height and weight and breadth on his side. Then, in contrast to his affability, another thought hit her with chilling speed. Gorgeous men sometimes capitalized on their good looks to lull women into their webs.

He rose and extended his hand. She stared at it for a moment as if it were a snake, then she finally grabbed it. Several impressions struck her at once. He had a firm grip. His gray eyes were flecked with brown. He smelled good, citrusy and clean. Probably better than she did.

Disconnecting her harness, she swatted his helping hand out of her way. "I'm fine. Thank you for your help. However, you're not supposed to be here. There are designated places—safer places—for visitors."

He brushed dust from her shoulder. "I'm already here. It's fate, trust me."

She lost the struggle to maintain control. "Will you stop saying that! You didn't rescue me, you idiot."

His face fell. "But I was prepared to. You've had

a terrifying experience. Isn't it possible you could be in shock, or hurt?"

She tossed her head in belligerent denial. "I'm not hurt. I'm not in shock. I've got two hundred and twenty feet of chute to roll up. Now go away."

"My name is Dennis Jorden," he said in a pleasant tone.

Glaring at him, she saw a rebuke in his eyes, tempered by a mock frown. She could practically hear him *tsk*!

"I, for one," he went on, "intend to remember everything we say to each other today."

"I can't imagine why."

He shrugged. "I told you, it's fate. You fell into my arms."

That earned him a short, derisive hoot. "Mr. Jorden, your short-term memory is faulty. I didn't fall into your arms."

He lifted a section of the chute, crunching it in his large fists. His mouth worked to suppress a grin. "I know, but it sounds better."

She couldn't believe she was debating the point with him, arguing as if he made sense. Then her gaze slid to her mangled chute. She yelped. "If you really want to help me, stop treating my chute like yesterday's newspaper."

He dropped it immediately and stepped back. "Show me the right way," he said solemnly.

"Forget it," she mumbled.

He paced along as she scooted around the chute's huge perimeter, grabbing handfuls of material and imitating her folding method. She treated it as a precious possession, handling it as if it were a cherished jewel. He wondered how her long, tapered, caring fingers would feel on his bare flesh. Caressing him.

As the thought flashed through his mind, she sent him a glare and told him again to go away.

He smiled. "When I'm satisfied you're okay. To put your mind at ease, I'm harmless. I don't bite. Unless it's a love bite."

Shaking her head, she flapped material over material, reducing the size of the chute. "I'm sure you have more important things to do."

"It's bad luck to fight premonitions. I feel connected to you. Besides, I love listening to your voice. It's low-pitched, throaty. Very sexy. What should I call you?"

"Mrs."

Dennis threw back his head, laughing. His gaze roved over her face, then settled on her lips. "Baloney. If you were married, you'd be wearing a wedding ring." He handed her another section of parachute.

She seized it from his hands. "Not necessarily. Some married women choose not to wear wedding rings."

"True, but you don't send out married vibes."

"There is no such thing as married vibes!"

He shrugged. "Let's not belabor the issue. You sure you're okay?"

"Positive."

"You might be sore." His gaze skimmed downward.

"Mr. Jorden, I don't give a fig about fate. I want you to go. I thanked you nicely and asked you nicely to go. I've run out of nice. In case you aren't aware of it, you crossed a runway to get to this field. Had a small plane come in for a landing or had one tried to take off, you could have endangered the crew's lives, and yours. There are safety reasons for visitors to remain in designated places. In short, you're not supposed to be where you're not supposed to be. Which is here."

He rocked back on his heels, studying her. "You're absolutely right. However, I'm responsible for you. You admitted you landed at my feet. That has to signify something."

She held the folded chute against her chest. "You're mixing this up with the Chinese custom. You didn't save my life. You nearly caused me to crash-land into you."

He frowned, and Roxy thought she had finally gotten through to him. Until he asked how long she had been jumping.

"Two years," she said, hoping he'd tire and leave. "Before you ask, it costs fifteen dollars a jump. On my days off I jump four or five times."

He scowled. "It's too dangerous. You could have been killed. More to the point, we can't do it together. Heights bother me. I get nosebleeds above the third floor. What else shall we do with our spare time?"

Roxy rolled her eyes. This handsome man with the killer smile viewed reality from a demented perch. "*We* have no spare time. Understand this, Mr. Jorden. *We* are not a scintilla of an item. *We* are not a couple. *We* are strangers. What's more, I could never see myself with you."

"How do you know? I'm kind to the elderly and young children. I never attend air shows or watch skydiving. I refuse to watch bungee jumping on television. My being here today is a fluke. So if our meeting isn't fate, what is it?"

She tipped back her head to meet his gaze. "It is immaterial to me whether you approve or disapprove of skydiving. I missed my mark. Wind shear, not fate, brought us together."

He tipped down his chin. "Since you obviously

think I'm a quack, let me dispel that by telling you about myself. I'm a forensic accountant. An account sleuth. I earn a good living. My future is bright. I'm a champion of women's rights. I have one sister who married a naval commander and lives in Norfolk, Virginia. I'm twenty-eight years old. I'm an ardent Giants fan. Housework doesn't faze me, although I can't say anything for it. I like kids, except when they're hellions. A year ago I bought a big old house that I'm in the process of remodeling. I mention my ownership to prove my stability. I graduated third in my class from the University of Pennsylvania's Wharton School of Business. I've never married. My health is excellent. So are my teeth and my vision. Whatever I'm feeling for you isn't my usual reaction to women. I'm basically a very private, low-key guy. Ask my friends the Ostners, or Marybeth Wynston. They'll vouch for me. Trust me, I don't normally come on to a woman like this. Therefore, since I'm as flabbergasted as you must be, I can only conclude there's a deeper meaning to my reaction. One we should vigorously pursue."

"You are nuts," she pronounced. "For the record, I'm not interested in asking your friends about you. I'm only interested in your leaving me alone."

"I understand your initial reaction, but now you're just being obstinate. What sort of training did you go through?"

She cocked her head. "Are you thinking of taking lessons?"

His look gave her his answer. "I'm trying to understand why a woman who is as pretty as you spends a glorious afternoon jumping for her life."

"Oh, for goodness' sake! Okay. We both know it's a waste of time, but if you leave, I'll answer." She didn't wait for him to agree but mechanically provided the information. "Initially the jumpmaster controls the static line. That's an umbilical cord. The line connects the parachute's opening mechanism to the airplane."

He chuckled. "Just like a mother nursing her baby."

She rolled her eyes. The man was insufferable. "After two successful jumps from eight thousand feet, you proceed to the next phase of training. Seven jumps from a height of ten thousand feet."

"You call that fun?"

"I sure do."

"I can think of better ways to have fun. Then what?"

"Then nothing. You interrupted me. On the seven flights, two jumpmasters accompanied me, making sure I correctly read my wrist altimeter and pulled the rip cord at three thousand feet. I also practiced turns, learned how to read ground speed and to land safely. And I would have landed safely today if you hadn't gotten in the way. Now leave."

A huge grin spread over his face.

"Did I say something funny?" Although he was batty, she had to admit he was the cutest bat she'd ever seen. That thought had her scowling again. It only proved the jump had rattled her brains.

He became even more amused. "Admit it, angel. We're made for each other. We absolutely should pursue this meeting. Oh, come on," he pleaded shamelessly. "Aren't you the least bit interested in following your instincts? Or do you limit yourself to the highs you say you get from skydiving? Didn't I take your mind off your scary jump? Didn't I make you feel better?"

His insanity aside, he had asked a fair question.

Roxy prided herself on honesty too. She did feel better. She knew that skydivers who experienced wind shear were often emotionally shook for hours after the dreadful experience. Some quit outright.

She held her hands out in front of her. They were steady. She touched her forehead. Cool. She felt . . . fine. Thanks to him. In his own crazy way he had succeeded in directing her mind away from fear—and to him.

He was gazing down at her, correctly reading her expression. "See?" he said. "I'm right. You don't have to admit it, though. That would be asking too much."

Dennis Jorden's smile could devastate a woman, Roxy thought, and she herself wasn't proof against it. Or his expressive eyes, which both calmed and speeded up her heartbeat at the same time. Old-fashioned goose bumps broke out on her arms. He packed a wallop of a sexual invitation, from the sensual curve of his lips to his enticing scent. *If she were foolish enough to be conned.*

She heard too many sad tales in her work. Along with her partner, Nina Arnouth—her jumpmaster's wife—she operated Safe Havens. Following the tragic death of her sister, Alice, and in Alice's memory, she had converted her home into a shelter for battered women. She and Nina hunted for jobs and permanent housing for the women, and scheduled counseling. Those women's horrifying stories were burned into Roxy's brain.

"Go away!" She raised her voice for emphasis.

"Roxy, are you okay? What's going on?" A deep male voice boomed out the question. She swiveled. Larry Creiger, the security guard for the airfield, was striding toward them.

Dennis answered, "She had a narrow escape. I ran over to help."

"I hit a wind shear, Larry, but I'm fine now."

Stopping beside them, Larry sized up Dennis. "Then why did I hear you tell him to go away?"

Roxy wet her lips. She was all right now, but for how long? She couldn't discount the possibility that Dennis Jorden might be dangerous, might try to follow her home. She knew nothing about him. Con men created false histories every day of the week. His smooth speech might settle another woman's doubts, but not hers. Not in her line of work.

Thinking of that, she answered Larry, "I asked him to leave. I work better alone. He's unfamiliar with jumping or folding chutes."

Larry astutely looked from one to the other. "Did you ask him to leave more than once?"

She avoided Dennis's gaze. "Yes."

"Dammit, angel," Dennis said softly. "Is that all you can say?"

"It's enough, mister," Larry said. "Wait here while I speak with Miss Harris. I wouldn't try anything foolish."

"It seems I already have," Dennis said as Larry led Roxy a short distance away.

Hearing the bitterness in his tone, Roxy shuddered. As if he had commanded her to look at him, she turned back. Their gazes met, clung. She studied his somber face, the firm line of his lips, and felt a wave of compassion for him. Looking at Larry again, she quickly told him what had happened, giving Dennis credit for trying to help her.

Satisfied with her explanation, Larry said, "I'll walk back with him."

But Dennis had already left.

# Two

In his second-floor office Dennis leaned back in his chair and opened a manila folder that contained a background check on Roxy Harris. After the way she had treated him, he should have been angry with her—and he had been until he'd calmed down. Judging the harrowing episode from her perspective, he acknowledged that he'd given her one or two scary moments. She scared the life out of him too. Then again, if she hadn't come barreling down out of the sky, he wouldn't have met his fiery angel. He planned to give fate a firm push, tip the scales in his favor.

He'd already had two more bits of good fortune. The first had been learning her name from the security guard. The second had been spotting a sign emblazoned on both sides of a red Pontiac parked near his car at Alexandria Field. SAFE HAVENS. DON'T TAKE ABUSE! PHONE ROXY HARRIS.

Within days of their fateful meeting his friend Jim Davis had called to ask him for a favor. Glad to be of assistance, he in turn had asked Jim to aid him in learning more about Roxy. Jim's stepfather, Gerry Matson, was a sergeant with the New Jersey State Police. Could Gerry help him learn more about Safe Havens and one of its owners, Roxy Harris? With both Gerry and Jim soon to be married, he earned their sympathy for his romantic plight. Gerry had said he'd see what he could do, and now, two weeks later, Dennis sat reading about his fiery angel.

Roxanne Harris had graduated from Glassboro State College with a major in early education. She'd taught kindergarten for one year. Why had she quit? he wondered. She operated Safe Havens, a shelter for battered women, with a partner, Nina Arnouth. Her parents resided in Toms River. Her sister, Alice, and Alice's husband, Tom, had been killed in an automobile accident a few years earlier. The husband's blood alcohol level had been three times above the legal limit.

Roxy had racked up three speeding tickets: two for going forty in a thirty-mile-per-hour zone; one for doing sixty-eight in a fifty-five-mile zone. For recreation she skydived. He could personally attest to the fact that she flew like a human bullet. He supposed she loved roller coasters, another death-defying experience he'd sooner stay away from.

He had expected to read she was voted Homecoming Queen. Instead she had worked in a daycare center after high school and during college. The report went on to say she marched in parades for various causes. He imagined her leading one with her beacon of red hair, waving a placard. He chuckled softly. He could also easily imagine her dumping the placard over his head. To help earn money for Safe Havens, she lectured before civic and other groups.

Money, Dennis mused. There might be an opening there. With Roxy needing capital for Safe Havens, he could offer her a monthly sum, providing she kept him abreast of how she disbursed the funds. Right up an accountant's alley.

He reached for the phone.

Sewing a patch on her parachuting coveralls, Roxy sat at her kitchen table. When she'd learned how much it would cost to mend her parachute, she'd squashed any lingering guilt that she might have treated Dennis Jorden unfairly. She would have to wait until the following month to fix her parachute. If she hadn't met Dennis—and she wished she hadn't!—she wouldn't be patching her coveralls. She'd still be skydiving. She'd have her freedom.

She finished her mending, then treated herself to one of the chocolate-chip cookies on the table. A local baker sold day-old bread to Safe Havens at a cheap price. A father of five, he threw in the cookies for free.

"Good. You're finished." Nina Arnouth breezed into the kitchen.

At five feet nine inches, she was three inches taller than Roxy as well as three years older. Her jet-black hair, deep brown eyes, and sultry skin tone contrasted with Roxy's red hair, green eyes, and porcelain complexion.

"Guess what?" Nina went on excitedly. "You received a phone call from Dennis Jorden."

"Oh, no!" Roxy wailed.

The story had fascinated Nina. She had hung on to every word, even asking Roxy to repeat sections of it, especially the physical description of Dennis.

"I'm dying to meet the man who was ready to sacrifice his life for you."

Roxy winced. "This isn't a joke. Dennis is a walking expense. If anyone sacrificed, I did. Unless I rent a chute, I won't be able to jump until Clarisse returns from Europe with my spare one. Dennis came away unscathed. What did he say he wanted?"

"I like him. He's got a marvelous voice. It sounds like a smiling caress. What could be more romantic than your meeting?" She sighed.

"Nina!" Roxy said sharply. "Why did he call?"

Nina straightened. "If you fail to get in touch with him—immediately, since I told him you were here—he'll assume you agree to see him tomorrow night. But he wants you to know he has a proposition for you—a business proposition."

"I'll bet."

Nina *tsked*. "He promised not to hold your ungrateful actions against you."

"That's big of him, considering nothing happened to him."

"That's the second part of the message. He's prepared to pay for your damages, though I admit he didn't sound that sorry about the parachute. He's afraid of jumping, isn't he?"

Roxy giggled. "Petrified. And he can send a check. A donation for Safe Havens."

"He said he's going to, providing you two get together. If you refuse, the deal is off. And before you do refuse," she added, warned by the look in Roxy's eye, "may I remind you we're continually tottering on the brink of bankruptcy?"

"In other words, charity begins at home," Roxy snapped. "His."

"You know, Roxy, one of these days a man will come along, and love will sock you between the eyes. When that day comes, I'm going to rub it in and say I told you so."

"You have a long time to wait," Roxy vowed. "I can assure you, Dennis Jorden isn't Mr. Wonderful. To begin with, he doesn't skydive."

"Skydiving is not the end-all criterion for marriage."

"It's a start."

"Baloney. What are you going to wear?"

Roxy looked down at her faded jeans and T-shirt. "This."

"I'm serious, Roxy. Show off your best assets. Have some fun, for goodness' sake. Your mother's right, you know. Skydiving is a lonely sport. Wear the green wrap dress. It matches your eyes. He'll love it."

"I'm not trying to make a good impression, and skydiving is not lonely." Nor, she added silently, did she want to see Dennis Jorden again. Still, he had offered a donation. She had no idea what sum he had in mind, but if it meant spending one evening with him to help Safe Havens, she would. And in that vein, maybe it would be wise to look her best. In the interests of furthering Safe Havens's goals, of course.

"Here's his number," Nina said, handing her a piece of paper. "Call him."

Roxy walked over to the kitchen wall phone and dialed, hoping he would be out.

He answered the phone himself. "Dennis Jorden," he said, sounding impersonal and business-like.

Nonetheless, his deep voice sent shivers down her spine. "This is Roxy Harris," she said quickly, before she lost her nerve. "All right."

"All right, what?" he asked, and his tone was now soft and intimate.

"I'll see you tomorrow night," she said, and hung up.

In his office Dennis laughed aloud. He was making great progress.

Two hours later, while Roxy was trying to make some sense of her own haphazard bookkeeping, Nina appeared in the office doorway, a young boy beside her.

"Hi," she said. "Meet Louey. His full name is Louis Miguel Esperanzo, but he prefers Louey. He's five. His mom's keeping an appointment with her social-service worker. They'll be staying awhile."

Roxy understood she had two more guests. The little boy had dark hair and huge dark eyes and wore scuffed shoes, frayed jeans, and a cotton shirt washed so many times, the original color had faded to a suggestion. Roxy would find a newer outfit for him in the box of clothing she kept. Right now, though, he looked as if he could use a hug and cookies. She gave him the first, then said, "Let's go see what we can find in the kitchen."

As they walked to the back of the house, he craned his neck, his inquisitive eyes absorbing everything. In the kitchen a card table sat beneath the window that overlooked the fenced-in yard. The table was laden with crayons and coloring books. From the yearning look in his eyes, it was clear he was dying to use the crayons.

"Louey," Roxy said, "Nina and I are about to have a snack. Do you think you could find room for cookies and milk?"

Louey nodded.

A little while later he handed her a drawing that filled her eyes with tears. He saw the world black. House. Grass. Sky. All were black. She cleared her throat. "Thank you, Louey."

He picked the spot where he wanted his picture to hang on the refrigerator door, then helped her set the table in the dining room for dinner. They were joined by Katherine Creeger and Allison Bruce, who had arrived the previous week with their children, one each. Both mothers were involved in nasty custody battles. With Louey and Maggie, the house was full.

Safe Havens needed help, desperately. For that reason Roxy called Bob, Nina's husband, that evening. Bob was her attorney, and she asked him to check on Dennis. He did, and called her back before lunch the next day. Dennis was Mr. Sterling Citizen with a fine reputation. Everything he'd told her at the airfield checked out. Even worse news for Roxy, both his office and his house were within a ten-minute drive of Safe Havens.

Still, she found her hand on the phone at least ten times that day to call him and cancel. Each time her hand retreated, common sense overruling her personal feelings. Safe Havens needed all the donations it could get.

With that uppermost in her mind, she took Nina's suggestion about what to wear. She chose her green dress, not only because it brought out the color of her eyes, but because the vertical-seam panels accented her slim waistline. She brushed her wavy shoulder-length hair until it shone, wearing it loose. She paid particular attention to her makeup, subtly shading her high cheekbones with blush, using dark mascara on her eyelashes and red gloss on her lips. She wanted to see Dennis's attention on her while she explained the need for shelters to aid battered women.

The last thing she did was to spritz herself with perfume.

Dennis arrived at her door at six wearing tan trousers, a crew-neck sweater, sneakers, and a drop-dead smile. He gave her a glowing once-over, then pursed his lips and whistled. Before she realized his intention, he completely disarmed her by lightly tracing her full bottom lip with one finger.

"I was right," he said as he handed her a single red rose. "The petals are as soft as you."

She swallowed hard. She'd gotten his attention all right. And darn him, he'd gotten hers! Once again she was impressed by his strong, manly features. Not that she trusted a single one. She was interested in his brain, not his body—which did wonders for his clothes. She told herself that three times before her breathing calmed down.

"Roxy, you look gorgeous." He sniffed. "You smell good too. And you have legs a Las Vegas show girl would envy. Next time I'll wear a suit."

She snapped out of her daze. "There is no next time. You're here for me to tell you about Safe Havens. I can do that in one session."

"Sorry. One session is information you'll *tell* me. I have to see things for myself too. Don't forget, I'm a forensic accountant. I keep my eye on people. If I like you—in a business sense, naturally—if I like your operation, and if we arrange for me to regularly see for myself that Safe Havens deserves continuous help, I'll donate a monthly sum."

Roxy fumed. He was using Safe Havens to get to her. The gall of the man. "I have to hand it to you, Dennis. That's some line you've got. All right, I have a few clarifying questions. Suppose you tell me why your sudden interest in Safe Havens? As I recall, you weren't too happy the day we parted."

The question did not take Dennis by surprise.

He had already thought out an answer she would have to accept.

"Why should I blame the messenger for the message? The fact that we got off on the wrong foot doesn't detract from my interest in helping women put their broken lives back together."

Roxy tapped the rose against his chest. "How come I don't believe you?"

He stopped the action by covering her hand with his. "Are you willing to take the chance I'm not serious? Are you willing to lose a generous donation? All I stipulate is that I check the way you spend my money. Surely, you can't object to a fair request. Or do you?"

She realized he was stroking her palm, sending delicious radiating sensations through her, and she wanted it to continue. She yanked her hand back. "It's not a fair request."

He leaned closer, closing his eyes for a second and breathing in her perfume. "Why not?"

"I don't do that for anybody. It's too time-consuming."

He shrugged and drew back. "Your choice. There's nothing left to say except good night."

She drew in a breath and let it out in an angry huff. If she let him go, she was letting money for Safe Havens slip through her grasp. He knew damned well she wouldn't do that, that she wouldn't turn down his help.

"All right," she said, "but don't for one second think I'm not on to you. Stop grinning, you trickster. For your information, I'm off-limits."

He smothered a chuckle. "Fair enough. You're far too unfriendly for me, anyhow. People who make appointments with me usually invite me into their homes. In case you haven't noticed, I'm still outside. So, given your suspicious personality, we'll conduct our business in a brief amount of time."

She tipped up her chin. "Now you're being sensible. For that I thank you. We can go into my office. I'll tell you whatever you want to know there."

He rocked back on his heels. "Over dinner."

Two words and they were back to ground zero. "Over dinner," she repeated.

"Over dinner."

She tossed her head, and her hands flew to her hips. "That's a date! I knew it, you weasel! This is a line full of rotten fish if I've ever smelled one. Look, I wasn't born yesterday. Why don't you stop wasting my time and admit the real reason you're here is because of me?"

"I told you why I'm here. To support your charity."

Roxy ground her teeth.

"Do you realize how many charities ask for money?" he went on. There was a note of rebuke in his voice, enough to keep her on the alert. "I'm in the process of investigating several charities for rich clients who need tax write-offs. A lot of people are fed up with charities that use most of their donations for managing expenses. I can't in good conscience offer a recommendation to a client unless I keep tabs on the charity."

*Or its owner,* Roxy thought. She calmly folded her arms over her chest. "Are you expecting clients to give monthly?"

Smart girl, Dennis thought. He felt the heat of her emotions, even though she struggled to repress them. "I make no promises. All I can do is give my best advice. Based on demonstrated need, naturally."

She rolled her eyes heavenward. "Of course."

"Shall we go?"

She swallowed a laugh. Dennis had handed her a perfect out, a way to shorten the evening. "We'll eat here."

He immediately shook his head. "I'd hate for you to cook. Let's go to a nice restaurant, then come back later."

She showered him with a beatific smile. "Nonsense. I made stew. I'm sure there's plenty." She put her hand on his arm. "Thanks to you, this is a much better idea. It fits in perfectly with your plans. This way you can see why we need money. After dinner you can read to the children."

"Read to the children?"

"Oh, thank you!" She clapped her hands in feigned delight. "Tomorrow you can tell your clients all about Safe Havens. Don't you think it's a good idea?"

*No, I don't!* "Wonderful. I never would have thought of it."

*I'll bet you wouldn't.*

On their way to the dining room, Roxy halted before a bulletin board hung in the hallway. "This will give you an idea of how we network. I post my daily schedule on the board. In addition to providing temporary shelter, Safe Havens directs women to the proper state and federal social and legal agencies. We coordinate with shelters in various states, and invite psychologists and even makeup artists to speak.

"Most women come here badly bruised. Stage makeup hides it. I keep a supply of samples. Part of getting better emotionally is seeing yourself healed physically."

Dennis paid strict attention to Roxy, barely glancing at the board with its job announcements, business cards, and names of women seeking to share apartments. He'd much rather watch Roxy in the flesh. In the very tempting flesh. And right now, he mused, she would cheerfully crack a placard over his head if she had one.

"I hope you like stew," she went on, continuing to the dining room. "Some nights it's more gravy than meat and vegetables. Tonight we're lucky. The butcher donated meaty bones."

"I love stew."

She glanced at him. "I'm so glad," she purred.

*You'd be happier if it were poison*, he thought, grinning as he followed her.

His smile faded when they entered the dining room. He was struck by the sudden quiet. It was clear his presence affected the two women and children seated at the table. Roxy introduced him to a thin blond woman named Katherine, another named Allison, her daughter, Bettina, and a little boy named Louey. His mother, Roxy said, would be joining them later.

The table was set with a linen tablecloth and candles, as if the women and children were honored guests. The crystal chandelier glistened over an arrangement of silk flowers, a china soup tureen, a woven china breadbasket, and a glass vegetable tray.

Family dinners in his house had always meant hearty food and hearty conversation. They had meant solving problems after dessert while his father smoked a pipe, using it as a little baton to quiet either his sister or himself if they were too boisterous, or to encourage one of them to speak. He had a good, supportive family. These women and children didn't.

He glanced at Roxy, lovelier than he had remembered, and he thought he had recalled each detail. Their eyes met. Hers shone with pride and courage. He stood motionless for a moment, staring at her, at the soft smile on her lips. How did she deal with the heavy burdens these people brought to her, maintaining her cheerful composure and not taking a break from her twenty-four-hour-a-day commitment?

"Are you a daddy?" Louey asked, breaking the silence.

Dennis looked at the boy. "Not yet. I hope to be one day," he said, his gaze returning to Roxy.

She touched his arm. "We're going to let you folks finish dinner," she said, and led him in to the kitchen. When the door swung shut behind them, he asked her what he had done wrong.

"Nothing," she said. "You're a man. A man represents a husband, a father. Louey and Bettina miss their fathers, and they need positive male role models. You can help by reading them a story after dinner. We can eat here in the kitchen, if you prefer."

He did. The cheerful yellow-and-white kitchen had a sturdy oak table and chairs, a card table heaped with books and crayons, with evidence of children's handiwork tacked on the refrigerator door with magnets. Herbs grew in pots on the windowsill. Cookie jars of various heights sat on the counter, along with books, a screwdriver, and washers.

Roxy followed his glance. "We're kind of loose around here."

"How many women do you see a day?"

She ladled the stew and carried bowls to the table. "It varies. Many contact me by phone, while others simply walk in. Sometimes I'll talk to ten a day, other times up to fifty. In this field everyone is overworked, whether it's the social-service counselors or those in private agencies. We do what we can, directly and by way of explanation. We work with religious groups too. We're grateful for any help we can get, directly or indirectly. The important thing is to effect change."

Dennis thought of his own job and life-style. To help him, his secretary, Patricia, ran his busy office. Another accountant would be joining his firm next month, and they would hire an assistant to take some of the burden from Patricia. He lived in a spacious home that he was converting to a bachelor's paradise. When he was a boy, he'd delivered newspapers to the house, never dreaming that one day he would buy it in a bankruptcy sale.

Roxy, on the other hand, had little help and no privacy. With various strangers living in her small house, privacy was impossible. The only place off-limits to the women and children, she told him, was her attic bedroom.

He reached for her hand. "How did you finance Safe Havens?"

Feeling his firm grip and the smoldering magnetism of his heated gaze, Roxy knew Dennis could prove to be a far more powerful force than fate. She had to struggle to remember what he had just asked.

"I inherited money from my sister, Alice." Despite herself, her eyes teared up. "My brother-in-law, Tom, killed her and himself by driving while drunk."

She sniffled, and when Dennis's grip tightened, she hung on, taking his comfort. "In an act of ironic justice, Tom died first. Alice suffered for a month. As his wife, she inherited his life insurance. When she died, I was her sole heir. It wasn't a lot of money but enough for me to start the shelter."

She gave him a wobbly smile. "I often tell my mother that pride serves the rich better than the poor. I do that to test my mettle. It works. I would never ask for anything for myself, but for the women and children, I'll ask for as much as I can."

"I'm so sorry about your sister," Dennis said quietly. "And very proud of you for the work you do."

Feeling a bit uncomfortable with the intense closeness of the moment, Roxy slipped her hand from his. She dabbed a piece of rye bread into the leftover gravy in her bowl.

"Tell me about the women who come here," he said, sensing it would help her to not discuss her sister.

His gentle voice seemed to enfold her. She found herself drawn to him in many ways, but her sister's marriage to an abusive man had made her extra cautious. She had vowed to remain single and focus her energies on Safe Havens, at least until it was on secure footing.

"They come from a cross-section of the culture. Their one common denominator is the rapidity with which their lives disintegrate, emotionally and, in many cases, physically. Their underpinnings of security disappear. Without a job or family support, their money runs out. Children are confused. Too many fathers toss aside their commitments. New Jersey law garnishees wages, but the process is long, and many fathers are hard to track down."

"How do you raise money?"

"We spread the word however we can," she went on, unobtrusively sliding her chair a bit away from him. "We rely mainly on donations from women's organizations, businessmen and women, established charitable organizations, and private donations, but we're going to have to do more to get the word out."

"How? What do you have in mind?"

"I don't know yet. I'm working on a few ideas, and so is Nina. Between us, we'll come up with something. The problem is, most people donate to larger, more established operations that can afford to mail out brochures to solicit money."

"What are your goals?"

She smiled somberly. "That's easy. I wish for the day there isn't a need for shelters like Safe Havens."

With complete clarity Dennis recognized the well of compassion that prompted her quick reply. Roxy was a born healer who wanted to cure the ills of the world. He put down his napkin.

"I want to pay for the damage to the parachute and your coveralls. They ripped because of me. What's the repair bill?"

Although she had told Nina she'd welcome his money, Roxy declined his offer.

"Listen to me," he said. "If you don't accept this, I'll just go out and buy you a new parachute. So save your breath and my bank account and take this check."

Reluctantly, she accepted the check, and her eyes widened at the generous sum. Despite his resolute tone, she said, "It's far too much. I can't accept this. Besides, you hate parachuting. You're scared of it. You wanted to know what we could do together."

Belatedly, she realized she'd just revealed that she remembered his exact words. A wicked grin tilted the corners of his mouth.

She blushed. "I—I didn't mean that."

Entranced by the display of emotions across her beautiful face, Dennis longed to put his mouth on hers, to bind her to him until she was breathless. But that would be the wrong move.

"I admit I'd rather cut the parachute up for handkerchiefs," he said. "Or sell squares for quilts at sewing bees. Please, don't make an issue of the money."

"All right," she said, then smiled sassily. "I'll invite you to watch my next jump."

He stifled a shout of laughter. If he had his way, she would never strap a jump rig to her back again.

"Wouldn't you like that?" she asked sweetly.

"Don't do me any favors. You know my thoughts on that subject."

Making sure she'd pocketed the check, he scraped his chair back and stood to clear the table. She wasn't used to being waited on and jumped up to help, but he waved her back down. He made himself at home in her kitchen, putting their dishes in the dishwasher, then pouring coffee for them. They drank in companionable silence. When he was through, he asked her to show him the rest of the house.

Roxy pushed aside the disturbing effects his nearness was having on her. She didn't want to encourage him, but for some reason her fingers itched to run through his golden hair, to feel its texture and weight. Women would die to have his coloring.

"Why do you want to see it?" she asked.

Why indeed? Dennis was undergoing a mental reorganization. He had come prepared to use Safe Havens as a means to get in her good graces. Until now his relationships with women had been temporary and without great emotional intimacy. Mostly he saw career-minded women who, like himself, wanted to get established in their jobs and keep marriage for later. But Safe Havens was an integral part of Roxy, and in just this one evening he could see his attraction to her ran much deeper than he thought. He wanted to see how she lived. He wanted to picture her in all the rooms.

"Roxy, you need money. I know people who might contribute to your cause or help you in other ways. But not even for you would I recommend a pig in a poke."

"Then you're not trying to date me?" she persisted.

He gazed into her compelling eyes. She was a lovely, spirited woman. He wanted to kiss her, make love to her, build a relationship with her.

"You know I am," he said.

"Thank you for being honest. I shall be equally direct. The other day I said we had nothing in common. I believe this still. We haven't, not to form a basis for—"

His narrowed gaze stopped her from ending the sentence. He focused on her lips, her breasts, then raised his eyes to meet hers. "Intimacy?" he asked softly.

She blinked, telling herself the meltdown she was feeling couldn't be allowed. She wouldn't be drawn into his web, no matter how tempting. "That is correct. My work comes first."

He leaned back and studied her. They could have been discussing the cooling weather, not the heat they were generating with each look, every nuance of motion. "Go on."

She coughed, clearing her throat. "That's it. Except for thank you." She clipped her words. "I'll accept your money and any assistance you might wish to give to Safe Havens."

"Now it's my turn to thank you," he said, matching her formal tone.

"And," she went on, her voice lifting happily as though she'd passed through a baptism by fire, "with a clear conscience, I can still refuse to date you."

He threw back his head and roared with laughter. The disgruntled look she gave him was so unconsciously provocative, he wanted to yank the little liar into his arms and show her what it could be like between them.

"You're chock-full of announcements, aren't you?" he said. "So tell me, pretty lady, what about fate?"

She grinned. "Phooey on fate."

He gazed at her mischievous eyes, her pert nose, the line of her elegant neck, then settled on her distracting, smiling lips. He slid his hands over her shoulders, deliberately bringing her forward as he tipped down his head. "If I were you, I wouldn't discount the power of fate."

# *Three*

Louey prevented Roxy from showing Dennis the rest of the house right then. He rushed into the kitchen and stopped abruptly, his gaze flying to Dennis, as if to make sure he was still there. It was clear he wanted to speak with him.

Dennis sat down to make himself less formidable. "My dad used to read me stories. How would you like me to read you and Bettina a story?"

Louey's eyes glowed. "Bettina's taking a bath. Would you read to me?"

"You bet."

Taking the child's hand, he followed Roxy into the den. She invited Louey to choose a book. He took a long time investigating the shelf of children's books, finally deciding on *Beauty and the Beast.*

Dennis winked at Roxy. "I love reading bedtime stories." His voice lowered to a nerve-tingling huskiness. "To women. Especially love stories. Shall I read one to you later? I promise to put my heart and soul into it."

"I'm sure you would," she said briskly, her own

voice too loud, "but I think you'd better stick to reading your stories to children. You're less likely to get into trouble that way. If you get my meaning?" She sent him a smug smile, then crossed to a chair and sat.

Dennis just chuckled. He sat on the couch and let Louey climb up on his lap. Sucking his thumb, the boy listened in rapt attention, poring over the pictures with slow deliberation and giggling when Dennis spoke in falsetto as he acted out Beauty's part.

Dennis halted to whisper loudly in Louey's ear. "Ask Roxy if she's enjoying my reading. Or does she think I ought to put more emotion into it?"

Like a good little parrot, Louey repeated the question.

Roxy couldn't help laughing. Looking around the room, she thought it had never felt cozier, more complete. Louey was glowing from Dennis's attention. He really was a rascal, using a child to get to her.

"Tell Dennis," she said to Louey, "that I'm going to bop him on the head with the book if he doesn't get back to his reading."

Before he could speak, Dennis covered Louey's mouth with his hand and finished the story.

Louey pleaded with Dennis to read it again. Roxy left the room, coming back with Katherine's six-month-old baby. Sitting in the chair again, she fed the infant her bottle.

Dennis stopped reading to watch, and Roxy felt the full impact of his searing gaze as she lightly rubbed the baby's back. Already he was knocking down the barriers of her preconceived image of him. She was learning that he was a man of many facets. As he sat silent, apparently fascinated by the miracle of life, she questioned the wisdom of feeding the baby in front of him, as if they were participants in a domestic play. She didn't want to foster a relationship with him. For many reasons.

Louey tugged his hand, drawing Dennis's attention back to the book.

After reading him the story for the third time, Dennis complained his throat felt scratchy.

"Will you read to me tomorrow night?" Louey asked.

"I promise," Dennis said. Louey threw his arms around Dennis's neck, and Dennis kissed him. Then Katherine came downstairs, and Roxy handed her the baby.

They were alone.

Dennis walked over to her and drew her out of the chair. "I enjoyed that. Mostly because you sat there taking time for yourself. You need that." He lightly stroked her cheek with the tips of his fingers, then combed her hair, just for the pleasure of touching it and seeing the light ripple through the shining strands. Then he lightly kissed her lips.

"Not all men are stupid," he said. "Most value their families. They'll do everything in their power to protect them."

"I know," she whispered, held motionless by his gentle caresses. He linked the fingers of one hand with hers, and it felt good. There were so few gentle male touches in her daily life. She glanced up to see him gazing down at her, his gray eyes darkening. There was knowledge in his eyes and a sureness in him that communicated from his every pore.

There was desire too.

She drew back abruptly. "We'd better take that tour now."

The upstairs consisted of a center hallway with

four clean, compact bedrooms. The beds were neatly made. Freshly folded towels hung on racks affixed to the dressers. Worn brown carpet covered the floors. Each room had a freestanding metal clothes closet and a folded cot.

"Space is at a premium," Roxy explained. "We try to be accommodating, though sometimes it's harder than other times. This week we're lucky."

He couldn't conceive of sharing his home with strangers. "How many bathrooms do you have?"

"Two. One up. One down. No one lingers. That's why Allison bathed Bettina right after dinner."

"I'd like to see your room."

She frowned. "Why? I'm not seeking funds for myself."

He had many reasons, each more personal, more intimate, than the last. "If I can tell my clients how you live, what you yourself have given up for others, it will help my presentation."

Roxy didn't know whether or not to believe him. She had been convinced he'd dangled a donation to Safe Havens as a ploy to see her. Until she saw him with Louey.

"All right. Watch your head," she added as they mounted the attic stairs. Behind her, she heard a thud, then a muttered expletive. "This isn't a very good idea."

Tucked under the eaves, the attic roof angled down from a central point. A low beam of light filtered into the room from downstairs, and she switched on a lamp.

Dennis stayed where he was. His head barely cleared the ceiling, providing he remained in the center of the room. Looking around, he saw she had transformed the space into a cozy refuge. Windows at opposite ends provided cross ventilation. Her slippers were at the side of her twin bed. The furniture consisted of a maple dresser, a lamp, a freestanding metal clothes cabinet, and a Queen Anne chair, its cushion covered with a material that had a cabbage-rose design. The chair looked as if it would break if he sat on it. Beneath one window that overlooked a weeping willow tree stood an open trunk overflowing with children's toys.

"Are these yours?" he teased.

Her chin lifted. "Every child receives a gift. We don't spend money frivolously."

"I didn't mean to imply you did. Souls need nourishing too."

He couldn't have said anything nicer to disarm her. She smiled. "I have a deal with the owner of a local toy company. These are seconds. The kids don't care."

"Is there anything you won't do for them?"

"Someone has to."

He followed her gaze to the picture on her dresser. The young woman bore a resemblance to Roxy. "Is that your sister?"

"Yes." She turned back to him. "Now that you've seen the room, we can go downstairs."

"I'd rather talk here."

"I don't entertain men in my bedroom. Even for charity."

He was tempted to confess he hadn't come for charitable reasons, but for himself, from a desire to see her again. He praised her work instead, refraining from adding that he thought she was wearing herself down. She would scoff at him, and she'd be right. From what she'd told him, she didn't have the operating capital to pay a staff, or move the shelter to separate quarters, thereby returning her home to her private use. He thought it awful she slept in the attic.

Her day started early and sometimes never ended. He'd asked her whether women called during the night. She'd said they did, and admitted that she hated to turn on the answering machine. Nina got the best of the bargain. Nina kept hours. Nina went home to a husband. And it didn't take a mathematical whiz to deduce, the more successful Safe Havens became, the more women and children would show up at her door, and the more taxing Roxy's life would become.

He found her watching him intently. He recognized the look in her eye, the mixture of pride and determination, as if daring him to voice his conclusions. If nothing else, Roxy, his fiery angel, fought for her beliefs.

"You're missing a bathroom up here," he said.

She laughed, a merry sound that bounced off the sloping walls. "I manage."

He was irritated that one tiny slip on those stupid steps could cause her to break her neck. He thought of his rambling house with its large rooms, four bathrooms, soaring fireplaces in the den and his bedroom, the modern kitchen. Roxy could use a house his size.

"You're lucky you haven't tripped and hurt yourself climbing those stairs in the middle of the night. Then where would your charity be?"

"I'm careful. No one is indispensable."

"You are to the people you've taken in, and to the others you help. It's a good thing you have Nina to relieve you of some of the burden."

"I know it, but when she becomes pregnant, she's got to take a leave of absence." At his curious look she explained that Nina had suffered three miscarriages. Her doctor had told her that with her next pregnancy she should not work at all.

Dennis threaded his hands through his hair.

"Roxy, you're a noble creature. But even honor-able, high-minded, lofty people can't change the world alone. You need help. Why not ask your board of directors? Surely they could help you out, donate a few hours a week?"

"What board? Nina, Bob and I are it. We don't have formal duties. We do whatever is necessary. Bob handles the legal work. I appreciate the time he devotes to tracing husbands and fathers to make them pay their legal share to their families."

Frustrated as much by the situations she de-scribed as by her overworking, Dennis sat down on the bed. Before he knew what was happening, the box spring fell to the floor, and the sides of the mattress shot upward. He was sandwiched in the middle, a stunned look on his face.

"What the hell!"

"It's fixable," Roxy said, quelling a laugh.

He exhaled roughly, struggling to get up. With nothing to grip, he couldn't.

"Here, take my hand," she said.

He grabbed and pulled hard. Now it was her turn to look surprised as she lost her balance and fell. She landed flat on top of him, their faces touching, their startled breaths mingling. Her hair formed a curtain around his face. She lifted her head, her eyes wide with shock.

The effect on Dennis was immediate. Electric. His gaze fixed on her ruby lips. "Roxy, I swear I didn't plan this."

She nodded, swallowing heavily. "I know. It's the bed."

He made no effort to move. His hands glided down her back.

"It's fate," he whispered.

"Please don't say that."

"Why? It's true." Bold desire was plainly written on his face.

His eyes seemed to swallow her up, and Roxy closed hers. It was not the question he had asked her but the answer she feared. Beside being cautious, if Nina became pregnant, the demands on her and her time would increase. Safe Havens needed her undivided attention.

Attention Dennis usurped for himself. She felt him nibble at her lips, felt his feather-light kiss, felt his restrained power. His supremely male body formed a single line with hers. Sighing, she allowed her hands to slip around his neck. She told herself she had no other place to put them. His hand curved around the nape of her neck, urging her head downward. She was flooded with a warm sense of well-being, of safety.

"Roxy," he murmured, "you should know I'm planning to kiss you very thoroughly. Unless you stop me now, you won't be able to."

She gazed into his eyes. With a little moan she pressed her lips to his, letting him take her on a sensuous tide. His hands traced her slender back and swept over her arms. Her body responded to his, pore by sensitive pore. Her fingers curled in his hair. In the deep recess of her mind she questioned how anything that felt so good, so right, could happen so fast to a cautious person. This wasn't like her. Then she stopped thinking.

All she wanted to do was feel, taste. To match dueling strokes of tongues. To relish him. On her bed. Where no man had ever been.

Dennis glided his hands along her spine. His body, which had been warming from the moment he saw her, heated to a flash point. In all his life he could never remember a more frustrating situation. He held a passionate woman in his arms and literally couldn't turn over. With excruciating pleasure-pain he felt her breasts pressing on his chest. Her sweet, panting breath whispered on his face. Fate had an ironic sense of humor. Even if he wanted to take it further, he couldn't.

He reluctantly ended the kiss. "I'm stuck. I've never been chaperoned by a mattress."

His words brought her embarrassingly back to reality, and she realized she had to move immediately.

"I'm going to lean on your shoulder to brace myself," she said. She did, and he winced. Thinking she'd hurt him, she quickly removed her hand. Instantly, she lost her balance once more.

Chuckling, his eyes alight with mischief, he locked his arms around her. "On the other hand, maybe we were meant to stay in your bed forever."

Cheeks flaming, she blamed herself for letting him think she was easy. Giving Dennis a cheap thrill wasn't on her agenda, for any price. If he thought she would offer a little something extra, he was dead wrong. "Bringing you up here was a bad idea," she muttered.

He laughed, and the rumble went from him to her. "Honey, bringing me up here was a great idea. When I phone you at night, I'll picture you safely locked up in your prison bed."

As if she'd been burned, she rolled over, tumbling onto the floor.

He immediately regretted the loss of her warmth, the sweet weight of her body, but realized this was best. Sensing her skittish nature, he knew he'd have to take it slow with her. Following her lead, he shifted to the edge of the bed. The back of the mattress rose and slapped him. "No one would believe this in a million years," he mumbled.

Despite wanting to maintain a semblance of dignity, Roxy couldn't. She giggled as he fought the mattress back. "Shall I call for help?"

"Don't you dare!" He slid to the floor, sat for a moment, then raised himself up on his knees. He shook his head, as if he couldn't believe he was crawling to the center of the room in order to stand up without killing himself.

"Roxy," he said, "I will never forget our meeting or our first kiss."

Since she was still reeling from that kiss, it took a moment for his words to register. "First?" She stood to face him.

"You really don't think I'm going to be satisfied by stopping there, do you? I've been wounded in action. I banged my head." He winked. "But you're worth it. Will you kiss it and make it better?"

"Dennis, everything's a joke to you, but not to me. We need to get something straight. We're different."

"Amen for that."

"There!" she said hotly. "You see what I mean? You're a big tease. I participated in one kiss under extraordinary circumstances. One is my limit."

He looked down at her. "Who are you afraid of? Me or you? Where did you come up with an arbitrary number? You enjoyed it. Don't tell me you didn't. If you want proof, come back with me to my house. We won't be interrupted."

"Absolutely not. I have no time to get involved. With you or any man."

"I'm not interested in other men. When will you have time?" he asked, no longer teasing.

"Not in the foreseeable future." She hoped he couldn't see the wild throbbing of her pulse.

He touched a finger to the pulse point in her

throat. "Angel, you've got your priorities all screwed up."

"They're my priorities. I didn't ask you to come into my life. I'm busy."

"So are most women. And men. Don't be afraid of me. All men aren't alike."

Without answering, she climbed down the attic steps, then descended to the first floor. Louey's mother, Maggie, met them in the hall. She was a pretty woman with a dainty figure and dark, soulful eyes like her son's. She nervously fingered the lapel on her tan suit.

Roxy welcomed her. "Maggie, how did it go today? Did you get the secretarial position?"

"No," Maggie said, obviously fighting dejection. "They said I need recent experience. How can I get recent experience if no one hires me? I'm running in circles. Where will Louey and I go? What will happen to us? I must be independent. I must."

Dennis injected himself into the conversation, ignoring the warning pressure of Roxy's hand on his arm. "Maybe I can help, Maggie. A new accountant will be joining my practice within the month, and I'm going to need an assistant. Can you use a computer?"

"No." She looked at him eagerly. "But I type fast, and my spelling is excellent. I can learn."

"Fine. Your references don't have to be recent."

Maggie's hope changed to gloom. Her shoulders slumped. She bit back tears. "I could try to get references, but it might be impossible. You see, I lost track of my former bosses when we moved here from Tennessee. Thank you anyway."

Dennis handed her his business card. "Come in tomorrow at nine. If my secretary Pat's satisfied, I'm sure I will be. She runs the office."

Maggie shyly took his proffered hand. She was

looking at him as if he were a god. "Why? Why are you doing this for me? You don't know me."

"You're a worthwhile person, so why wouldn't I? References are important, but so is judgment. Louey sat on my lap when I read him a story tonight. Since he's a nice little boy, you must be a good mother." He felt increasingly awkward at her glowing expression. "Don't make this more than it is. I'm not promising you more than an interview. We'll take it from there."

Roxy was touched by Dennis's largess. "You know nothing about her," she said after a choked-up Maggie left. "Why did you do it?"

He shifted his weight. "There are times when it's wise to play your hunches. What I said about Louey was true. Pat will review her skills. She's fair."

In a spontaneous gesture of gratitude that caught Roxy completely by surprise, she threw her arms around Dennis's neck and kissed him. He cupped her buttocks, bringing the heat of their bodies into consuming contact even as he fused his mouth to hers. She yielded to the sweet invasion of his tongue.

"Roxy," he said at last. "We're going to have to do something about this."

"We're in the hall, for goodness' sake," she weakly protested.

He stared at her pink cheeks and her sparkling sea-green eyes. Turning, he led her to her office and shut the door behind them.

"We're no longer in the hall. The least you can do is finish what you start."

More than a little rattled, she said, "I have no idea why I allowed you to kiss me."

"A gentleman should never point out it was the lady who initiated the kiss. Don't apologize. I enjoyed it. I freely offer my body for your entertainment, but I caution you, I'm a man of healthy appetites."

"Go home."

"Not yet. Show me your books so I'll have an idea of how much you need on a monthly basis."

Glad to shift topics, she hastily handed him several large envelopes.

"What's this?" he asked.

"Records."

He dumped the contents onto the desk. "If I didn't know better, I'd swear a rank amateur accountant allowed a rank amateur bookkeeper to get away with this nonsense. What happens if you lose these scraps of paper? They're not stapled to pages in a date book. How do you prove your expenses? Take a piece of advice, Roxy. If you're throwing good money away on the person responsible for this lousy bookkeeping, fire him or her. If it's a volunteer, get rid of him or her. This could land you in serious trouble. Suppose you're audited? You'll need to furnish proofs of your expenses, donations, everything."

Her gaze skittered away, and she felt her cheeks grow warm. "I can't."

"Can't what?" he asked more sharply than he intended, but he was disgusted. He kept meticulous records.

"I can't fire the bookkeeper or the accountant." Her voice grew lower.

He frowned. "Why not? Don't tell me a relative you feel sorry for does it?"

"Not exactly."

"What 'exactly'?" he persisted. "I know you have a heart of gold, and I suspect you wouldn't squash a fly, but keeping scrupulous records is imperative." He found a phone bill. "How do you know the personal from the business calls?"

"I recognize the numbers."

"Five years from now, seven years from now? This would drive me crazy. I was serious when I said the IRS could audit you anytime. Let me see last year's tax return. Maybe then I'll get a better idea. You know, there are simple established methods for posting expenses."

She swept past him toward the door. "I'm not trying to drive you crazy. It's not necessary for you to get involved. You already know what we do. Why isn't that satisfactory?"

"Roxy, I'm trying to help you."

Giving in to his obvious determination, she returned to the desk, pushed him aside, and opened a drawer. "It may be in here."

He gently but firmly removed her hand, then pulled the drawer out and emptied it on top of the desk. Packages of gum, pink and blue pacifiers, snapshots of children and women, and tiny plastic treasure chests tumbled out, along with pencils, paper clips, colored markers, rulers, and a notebook.

He lifted the lid of a tiny green plastic chest. "What's this for?"

"It's for the tooth fairy." She grew belligerent when his brows rose, and snatched the little chest from him. "I give the kids a quarter when they lose a baby tooth."

He laid two fingers across her lips. "Roxy, you're something else. You worry about kids losing teeth when you could lose your tax-exempt status. You're a woman of diverse talents, but I seriously doubt that you can assuage the IRS by giving the agents a tooth-fairy toy chest. Where's last year's tax return?"

She scooped up the contents on the desk, dumping them back into the drawer. "Dennis, you must be tired. I am. I'm not in the mood to go over tax returns or to answer questions."

Suspicion rose in him. He gave her a steady, sharp look. "Roxy, who does your bookkeeping?"

She let out a deep breath. Avoiding his eyes, she confessed: "I do."

He smiled as if she'd just handed him a present. "I think you're wonderful. I'll be back tomorrow night."

"What for? I told you I'm busy."

"I'm returning," he said in final tones, "to set you up with a simplified bookkeeping system. When I have time, we can alternate keeping the books. Safe Havens is a financial disaster waiting to happen."

"Tell me something I don't know," she muttered. Or something Bob didn't tell her each time he saw her drowning in red ink.

Dennis put his arm around her shoulder. "Don't take it so hard. I'll rescue you, just like I tried to do before. Exactly the way I intend to do from now on."

"Don't say that," she wailed. "I'm not helpless."

"Of course not."

She shot him a belligerent glance. Her mood was definitely sinking. She knew she was smart. It was just that she despised wasting time keeping records. Bob had urged her to get rid of the envelope system too. She liked it, though. Once a year she sorted the receipts into piles according to category, placed them in separate marked envelopes, and handed the whole thing to an accountant. Who invariably rolled his eyes. If she allowed Dennis to set up a new system, in good conscience she'd have to use it. Moreover, based on his generous offer to take some of the record keeping off her shoulders, he had figured out a way to stay in her life.

"I'm an organization fanatic," he said, pushing his point. "You aren't. It's a wonder you know where things are."

"I am organized in my own way. I resent you saying I'm not. I couldn't run Safe Havens otherwise. It's just that I'd rather walk on broken glass than waste time keeping books."

He held up his palms in a gesture of surrender. "Easy. I wasn't trying to insult you. If you hate his job, why doesn't Nina do it?"

"She'd rather jump out a window. I don't know how people can slave over columns of figures every week when it's just as easy to do it once a year."

He chortled. "There, that proves it's fate. We complement each other. I was fated to set you up with a better record-keeping system."

"How do you do that?" she demanded.

"What?"

"Put a spin on everything I say to make it come out your way?"

He kissed the tip of her nose. "*Our* way, Roxy. Besides, I have to read to the children. I'm also going to set up the jungle gym I saw lying on the ground out back. It's my intention to show you I'm indispensable. And I'd appreciate your help in getting this romance going. Sleep tight, sweetheart."

Staring at the door after he left, she realized he didn't need any help. He was doing fine. If anyone needed help, she did.

# Four

The following morning the peeking sun had barely painted the sky when Roxy's bedside phone shrilled. She grabbed it on the second ring, hoping it wasn't another emergency call. She had received two during the night. Getting an uninterrupted night's sleep seemed like an unattainable dream.

"Mmmmm?" she answered.

"Good morning," Dennis said.

His deep male voice brought her vibrantly awake. She imagined him unshaven, his blond hair mussed, his leg propped at an angle on his bed. Before she could complete the intimate picture further, he cheerfully asked her if she had slept on the floor.

"No. As a matter of fact, I slept on your side of the bed," she teased.

"In that case," he countered on an exaggerated sigh, "you had a restless night. Now don't you wish I'd been there to provide comfort, or to cushion your delectable body in case the stupid bed broke again?"

Roxy recalled his strong, steadying hands, his clean breath, his strong chest, and the ironlike vise of his legs. A blush rose to her cheeks, and she half expected to see him beside her.

"Don't be silly," she said. "Sleeping on the floor is good for the spine."

"Personally, I'd prefer snuggling with you."

She pictured him rising from the bed, gesturing with his expressive hands to make his point. She smiled at his persistence. "Don't you ever give up?"

"I can't be rude to the Fates. Those three goddesses have been exceedingly kind to me."

She laughed. "But what about me? Why haven't they been kind to me?"

"Roxy, don't you know by now, you're the one who can answer that question? I think you need a friend, a protector, and, if you allow me the honor, a lover."

His switch to seriousness startled her. She imagined the lines of tenderness around his mouth. Her heart gave a nudging beat, as if to warn her to restore the conversation to a bantering lightness.

"And you?" she asked, disregarding the clanging warning bell from her core of self-preservation. "What do you need?"

Her sister's likeness stared at her from its silver frame. Alice had believed she was marrying a good man. In the beginning of her marriage she had known love, but she'd paid dearly for it when her husband showed his true colors. Roxy wouldn't let the same thing happen to her.

"I need exactly what you need," Dennis answered. "If two people are blessed to blend into one spirit, one soul, they nourish each other." He reverted to his usual casual tone. "Speaking of nourishment, what time shall I pick you up for dinner? The stew's on me tonight."

"I agreed to see you tonight on business. Not for a date."

"What do I have to do? Jump out of an airplane?"

She giggled. "Shall I be your jumpmaster? Help you out the door?"

"No, I'm not crazy." His tone was mildly horrific. "I was speaking in the abstract. I told you I get nosebleeds above the third floor."

She sat up, cross-legged. "How do you see clients with offices above the third floor?"

"We meet in the basement."

She chortled. "I still won't go out with you tonight."

"All right. If it makes you feel better, I'll see you after dinner. I appreciate a woman who saves my money."

She heard the rustle of paper and what sounded like a metal cabinet shutting. "Where are you?"

"I'm at the office. I've got an important case coming up for a client in California. I'll be called to testify."

"When are you going?"

"In a week or two. I'm waiting to hear. Are you going to miss me?"

"What do you think?" she teased, avoiding the answer and hanging up.

Leaning back in his office chair, Dennis let his smile fade. He'd enjoyed speaking with Roxy, despite her saying she had agreed to see him only for business reasons. Even if her bookkeeping was meticulous, he would have dreamed up a reason to see her again. He could still see her startled, wide-eyed expression when she'd fallen on top of him the night before. And then the instant when it had turned to trust, and more. She was an inquisitive woman, and a woman of passion. She had kissed him, whether from hunger or curiosity. It didn't matter to him. It was a beginning. What had surprised him—stunned him—was his volatile reaction to her. He had kissed many women, but none who set him afire the way Roxy did. Her wonderful scent had enveloped him, even as her hair had formed a tent of privacy over them. Kissing her was close to perfection. It would have been stellar if he'd been able to move.

She had kissed him impulsively when he'd offered Maggie a job interview. Roxy must have surprised herself as well as him. He'd seen awe and wonder in her eyes when they drew apart. Then, swiftly, protectively, she'd reverted to type, shutting him out from her inner self. But not before he'd seen her confusion. He doubted she knew that by dismissing the kiss she had conveyed a wealth of information. It gave him hope even while it filled him with frustration to know that he'd pass Roxy's line of defense only if he maintained a casual, nonserious attitude.

He swore to exercise patience. After all, he had no alternative. He sincerely believed the Fates had planned their meeting.

Roxy hurried out of bed, Dennis's voice still echoing in her ears. The mere suggestion of fate drawing them into each other's arms had started a chain reaction of charged nerves from her head to her toes. When she'd met Dennis, she'd categorized him as a madcap, a Don Quixote with a sense of humor. Now he was doing his best to alter her perception. When he wasn't throwing fate at her, she enjoyed his whimsical good nature. But then he would spoil it by saying all she had to do was agree to give herself over to fate—and him—and *voila!* Life would be wonderful.

She didn't believe that, but, being the honest sort, she had to admit their kisses had been wonderful. When she'd fallen on top of him, his strong arms had trapped her like tender vises. Whatever he did to stay in shape worked very well. Too well. His body had been rock-hard and almost unbearably enticing beneath her. He had nuzzled her lips, caressed her neck, kissed the sensitive soft spot beneath her ear. He'd triggered an avalanche of emotions that zinged her right down to her curling toes. She had kissed him to satisfy her curiosity. Now that she had, she could and would conduct herself with professional decorum.

In short, no brief fling. No temporary romance. However appealing.

She stepped into her bedroom slippers, put on her robe, and peered out the window to get an idea of the day's weather. She selected a tan suit with a white blouse to wear for her brief talk before the Rotary Club that day. This morning she would update her notes and prepare a chart to take with her to the luncheon. The Rotary and other well-known organizations traditionally supported their favorite charities, so advocacy and education were important.

After showering and applying her makeup, she dressed, adding a pair of pearl earrings. She stopped in her office for a sheet of oaktag, a ruler, and colored markers, which she carried into the dining room to prepare a visual for her little talk.

She met Maggie in the hall as she was leaving for Dennis's office and wished her luck. "Don't worry about Louey. He'll be fine with me. If you're not back when I leave, Nina will watch him."

Nina joined her in the dining room about half an hour later. She slipped into the seat opposite Roxy, setting a stack of postcards in front of her. She glanced at her watch, then started to address the top card. "Maggie's interview should be under way by now. Not many people are as kind as Dennis was to her. We both know how difficult it is to land a good job. Were you by chance thinking about him when I walked in?"

Roxy looked up from her task. "Is that a guess or am I transparent?"

Nina, looking regal, her abundant hair braided, kept a noncommittal expression. "A little of both."

Roxy bit her lower lip. "I hope it works out for her, but what are we going to do? We've got to come up with ways to increase donations. Have you any ideas?"

Nina wished she did. "We're trying too hard, and our brains are fried. Personally, I'm hoping for a magical solution. Or"—she winked—"we can ask Dennis to get help from fate."

"You sound like him," Roxy muttered.

"Whatever works. What did Dennis say when you told him you keep the books?"

Roxy chuckled. "I thought he'd have a fit. Talk about how to get Dennis serious. He said they're a disaster. He said I should fire my accountant. Then he turned my messy bookkeeping to his advantage. He's gallantly offered to rescue me. I must say, he's persistent."

Nina toyed with her pen. "I like a man who knows *who* he wants. Bob wants to meet Dennis when he comes to go over the books. But that's business, not pleasure. We're hosting a small dinner party next Saturday night. Why not ask

Dennis to come as your date? From what you've told me about him, he sounds ideal."

"For someone else, not for me."

"How would you know if you refuse to give him a chance?"

"I don't have to date him to know I can't be interested in a man who blanches whenever he hears the word 'skydiving.' I trust my inner voice. It tells me to choose a man with whom I have mutual interests. I'm delighted Maggie likes him. I'm thrilled Louey loved it when Dennis read him a bedtime story. I like Dennis. It's hard not to, but that's a far cry from encouraging a relationship with a man who thinks fate brought us together."

"Roxy, that's not the first time you've said you're attracted to him." Nina put an addressed postcard in a separate pile.

Roxy shrugged. "Of course I'm attracted to him. So what? Physically, he appeals to me. I'm not blind or immune to his potent sex appeal. The man's got a terrific body."

She wouldn't make the same mistake her sister had, falling for a man because he was physically appealing. Still, those weren't pecks she and Dennis had exchanged, but full-fledged wallops of sensory assault. The man was sneaky, following up with an early morning phone call to make sure she didn't forget him. She wouldn't, not with the phenomenal circumstances of their meeting, but she would dismiss the lingering effects of his kisses.

Nina got up to stretch. She mentioned an appointment with her fertility specialist, then asked, "If you're afraid to take chances, how will you find a husband?"

Roxy checked the amount of grocery money in her wallet. "I'm not looking for one. Getting involved is the last thing on my agenda. Safe Havens comes first. Once it's on secure footing, I'll think about my love life."

Nina grew serious. "Roxy, is there a connection between your putting your personal life on hold with Bob and me trying to get pregnant?"

Roxy gathered her things. "Don't be ridiculous. You know me. I'm the one-thing-at-a-time type." She only partially lied.

Dennis's secretary, Patricia, knocked on his door, then entered. He put down his pencil and pinched the bridge of his nose. Setting aside the computer-printout sheets he'd been studying, he smiled at her.

"Is there something wonderful in those printouts?" she asked. "You're in an uncommonly good mood today."

His smile broadened. He'd been friends with Pat and her husband, for years, so he and his secretary had an informal working relationship.

"It's not the printouts," he said. "It's a woman named Roxy Harris. She runs the shelter where Maggie and her son are staying. How did Maggie do?"

"She's a timid soul, but I like her. She passed the typing test with flying colors, and even showed some aptitude on the computer. She's bright. If you're asking, I say hire her. She told me a little about herself. Given the opportunity, she'll be a loyal asset. If it's okay with you, we can lend her a lap computer to practice on at home."

"That's good enough for me."

They strolled down the hall to where Maggie waited nervously in the reception area. Dennis's offer of a job wiped away her tension and brought a wide smile to her face. Then, overwhelmed by the swift turn of events that had changed her life from despair to hope, she began to weep.

Dennis protested gently, assuring her she'd earned the job on merit. He felt uncomfortable, unused to watching a woman sob. How did Roxy stand it? he wondered.

Maggie wiped her face, inadvertently removing the makeup that covered the bruise on her cheek, inflicted by her husband. Dennis and Pat exchanged swift glances. He clenched his teeth to keep from cursing aloud. No wonder Roxy's heart went out to these women.

"Who's caring for Louey?" he asked.

Mention of her son returned the smile to her face. "Roxy. She's been so good to me, to everyone. She drives herself, though. I understand she's been doing that for a long time. She'll wear herself out if she's not careful."

He could agree with that.

"Today, for instance," Maggie went on, "Roxy's meeting with several employment counselors in the morning. Then there's the Rotary Club luncheon. I can't remember what else . . ."

Dennis's ears perked up, though he kept his expression impassive. Until Maggie's remark, he had wished he hadn't agreed to attend the Rotary Club luncheon at the invitation of one of his clients. As eager as he was to get to work on a case involving a whopping ten million dollars of hidden profits, he now couldn't wait to go to the luncheon. Interesting that they both were attending it. . . .

Fate.

Roxy lifted her foot from the gas pedal. She resented creeping when she was in a hurry. It seemed as if everyone who drove was behind the wheel of a car that day just to prevent her from arriving at her destination early. She liked to have time to look over her notes.

She rolled down her window, telling herself to relax. Tomorrow she would take her parachute in for repairs. Jumping would relax her. Providing she didn't hit wind shear again.

Reaching the restaurant at last, she parked her car, checked her hair and lipstick, then walked briskly into the restaurant, her chart under her arm. Gladys Harter, a friend of hers who owned a lingerie store, waved to her, indicating an empty seat at her table. Roxy nodded.

"You don't want to sit there," a male voice whispered in her ear. "I saved you a seat."

Dennis. She whirled around. She had jumped when he'd touched her, not from fear but from the electricity of his touch.

"Dennis, what are you doing here?" He looked splendidly sexy in a white shirt, burgundy sport jacket, and gray trousers.

"I'm following our destiny, sweet. I told you it's fate."

"Fate, my foot," she said, though she felt the soft persuasion in his voice. "Who told you I'd be here today?"

"Maggie. I'm here as Steven Ostner's guest." He sniffed her neck. "You smell delicious. Nice suit too. It's the right look. Professional. Important." He squeezed her arm. "Personally, I prefer you in the dress you wore last night. Hiding your curves in a suit is a criminal offense."

A ripple of pleasure ran through her. She felt deliciously warm. Feminine. Appealing. "Thank you, but I promised a friend I'd sit with her."

His face fell. "All right. I'll see you later."

As she walked away, Dennis remained standing there, watching her appreciatively. She was seductive, alluring. His. She just didn't know it yet. He returned to his table and sat down next to Steven. A client and friend for years, Steven published the *State Press*.

During the meal Roxy carried on an animated conversation with her friend. But often she looked up to see Dennis staring at her. His eyes were thoughtful, serious, with none of his usual warm light.

In fact, Dennis was fuming. The portly man seated on his right was lucky he didn't punch his lights out. Before Roxy had even given her speech, the man was telling Dennis that Roxy was a self-serving, money-hungry woman. A con, who wanted to live rent free on donations.

The man lathered butter on his bread. "That's not all. You open a shelter in a residential neighborhood, you lower the property value. It attracts riffraff."

Dennis put down his knife. He thought of Maggie and of Louey. "Do you know Miss Harris or anything about the kind of men who batter their wives?" he asked tightly.

"I don't need to. That's a private affair. I know Harris's type, though. I know she's out for herself."

Dennis clenched his teeth.

"Watch the way she works the audience," the man continued. "She'll sound like a preacher on the stump."

Dennis had no patience with close-minded people, especially with Roxy's reputation involved. "Why not listen to her speech before passing judgment?"

Alerted by Dennis's censorious tone, the man frowned at him. "I haven't seen you here before. Are you a member?"

"Harvey," Steven said, leaning forward. "Dennis Jorden's my guest. I agree with him, by the way."

Before Harvey could respond, the program chairperson introduced Roxy. In a steady, effective voice she cited how domestic violence affected not only women but children. She told the audience that many children ended up in the foster-care system, and that cost the taxpayers money. "We as a nation," she continued, "cannot morally or financially afford to turn our backs on abused women and children. The women have done nothing wrong. With your help we can give them back their dignity, their self-worth. All it takes is a start. They don't wish to be a public burden. Safe Havens is devoted to helping them achieve this goal. In turn, we need your help."

Dennis's heart pounded with pride. Roxy's eyes sparkled with passion as she spoke. She enchanted him, from the tip of her shiny head to her toes. He thought of her scent, of how she had been visibly irritated with herself for spontaneously kissing him, then laying the blame for it on him!

He grinned. He could become a habit!

Roxy sat down to a polite smattering of applause.

"She's got an insurmountable task," Steven said to Dennis. "Safe Havens needs professional PR. The public is inundated with requests for charitable donations. She's running a peanut operation."

"How about doing a feature story on Safe Havens?"

Steven considered that for a moment, then nodded. "I'll bring it up to my feature editor. Readers need to focus on a personality. If we had an angle, it would help."

"Roxy skydives."

Steven raised his brows, looking at Roxy with renewed interest. "Gutsy, isn't she?"

Dennis chose not to answer.

The luncheon meeting drew to a close. Dennis kept an eye on Roxy, hoping to speak to her before she left. She'd already risen from her seat.

"How important is she to you?" Steven asked, following his gaze.

Dennis rubbed his chin. After a moment he said, "I'm not sure. All I know is that the more I see her, the more I want to be with her."

"That's important," Steven said. "Shouldn't you be hurrying out to speak with her instead of standing around with me?"

"I'm your guest." He craned his neck to see Roxy go out the door.

"I can see that means the world to you," Steven said dryly. "Quit standing on ceremony and find the woman before she leaves."

Dennis didn't need to be told twice. "Thanks. I'll call you."

He caught up with her in the parking lot. "Hey, you were leaving without saying good-bye. I wanted to tell you that you were great."

She shook her head, a hand raised in protest. "Don't be kind. I wasn't great. I wasn't even good. I did terribly. Not one question. Nothing. They tuned me out. I failed."

Her shoulders slumped. She looked so woebegone and dejected, and sounded so discouraged, he told her what Steven had said to lift her spirits.

"I'll believe it when I see it in print," she said. "Twice newspapers have promised us a feature story. Twice it hasn't happened. Thanks for trying, but I've got to come up with other ways to get the public's interest."

"Hey. That doesn't sound like my crusader."

Roxy's head was buzzing, and she was aware that in her present mood, she could easily talk herself into laying her head on his chest, wrapping her arms around his waist, and feeding on his warmth.

"Dennis, I'm not your anything."

His gaze lowered to her lips. "Your kisses tell a different story."

"They're through talking."

"You need cheering up. Come with me a minute."

"I've got four stops, then I'm going to the supermarket."

Refusing to take no for an answer, he led her to his car and opened a rear door. "Get in. Please." He slid in beside her and closed the door.

She sighed. "I'm in. What do you want?"

He drew her into his arms. "Nothing. I just want to be here for you."

She went still, savoring his strength, his silent comfort. After a while she felt him stir, felt his lips graze her forehead. Tension of another sort flowed through her. A part of her brain recognized she was melting.

"Don't," she murmured. "I'm vulnerable."

He chuckled. "That makes two of us."

A rush of liquid fire streamed through her. "Dennis, I have to go. I'll be late."

"Mmmm. The last time I necked in a car, I was in college."

She put her hand on his chest. "We're not necking."

He tilted up her chin and kissed her cheeks, the corners of her mouth. "Sure we are. Roxy, we're at the far corner of an empty parking lot. Trees hide us from the road, and there's a field on the other side of us. So yes, we're about to do some serious necking."

He lifted her onto his lap, supporting her back with his hand. Then he lowered his head, pressing his lips to hers, and Roxy, who had been tense and upset, stopped thinking. Dennis was giving her the kind of kisses she dreamed of and fantasized about. Kisses of primal possession, of male promise. A soft moan of desire escaped her as she held him fast.

"I think we're going to have to continue this on a bed, sweetheart," he murmured against her neck.

She jerked herself upright, staring at him. His eyes crinkled with tender amusement.

"You had no right to do that," she said primly.

He kissed her full on the mouth. "Damn, you've got that routine down pat."

"I don't know what you mean. I didn't take advantage of you. You took advantage of me."

He laughed. "The same way I took advantage of you in your bed? By the way, how is the sandwich?"

"Don't change the subject."

"Okay. I kissed you because I wanted to make you happy. As happy as we started getting yesterday before you stopped me."

She patted her hair, straightened her skirt. "Correction. We mutually decided to quit. As for just now, you wanted to make *you* happy."

His lips twitched in amusement. "True. Can I help it if it works both ways?"

"Do you realize we have nothing in common? And if you say sex, I'll belt you."

"I'm getting tired of that excuse. Try another. How can you be so impetuous in the air and so damn cautious on the ground? You plan your day down to a T. You guard your emotions. I know you want me. I can feel it in your response. In the way your pulse speeds up."

And she had felt the warmth of his body, his strength, his heady caresses. Now she read the determination in his eyes. "I will not let it matter," she said, and got out of the car.

He followed her and sighed gustily, managing to sound as annoyed as he felt. "I'll see you tonight around seven. Have the books, or should I say envelopes, ready."

"I'll dump them on the desk."

"You're something else," he said, restored to good humor by her impudence.

"That's what all the men say," she tossed over her shoulder as she walked to her car.

"It's fate!" he yelled.

"Phooey on fate," she called back.

Her heart pumping, Roxy sped out of the empty parking lot. It wasn't fate causing her to lose her equilibrium. Dennis, the devastating charmer, attracted her as no man ever had. Pure unadulterated sexual intoxication, which she'd foolishly thought she had under control. Common sense dictated she relegate him to the status of forbidden fruit. One succulent bite and she lost all common sense, even her sense of propriety. Necking in his car in broad daylight was a prime example of why she should keep him at arm's length.

After stopping at the food market, she drove home, her new resolve still firm. Within minutes of arriving there, she received a phone call from Shannon O'Brien, a widowed mother of four. Fire had destroyed her house, and her late husband's insurance company was holding up her claim. She had a place to stay that night, but her funds were running low. A friend had told her of Roxy. "I know this isn't your normal concern, but could you help us?"

Roxy invited her to Safe Havens. "Come tomorrow. We'll figure something out."

"Roxy, this isn't a case of battering," Nina said when Roxy told her after she got off the phone.

"The O'Briens must have family, friends, someone. We've got to draw the line. We can't be all things to all people. We're going to have to be more businesslike in our approach, and you're going to have to keep regular hours. As it is, you're bursting at the seams."

"I'm fine," Roxy said. "You'd have done the same thing. You're trying to get pregnant because you love kids. Could you turn away four children? It won't be for long. We'll use the church list and find her a place to live."

"Where will you put them in the meantime?"

"I'll give Shannon and one of her kids my bed. Her baby can sleep in a crib. The other two we can put on cots downstairs. It'll work. I'll bed down in a sleeping bag in my office."

Nina shook her head. "You make me feel guilty. What time is Dennis coming tonight? I've got to tell Bob."

"Seven," Roxy answered.

"Okay. I'll go get dinner started. By the way, your mom called."

Roxy's mother worked part time in a hardware store. A redhead like her daughter, she had bright blue eyes and a sunny disposition. Her interests ran the gamut from Japanese bonsai plants to deep-sea fishing. Her main interest, though, was Roxy's happiness, which to her meant the stability of a good marriage.

"When are you coming to see us?" her mother asked when Roxy called.

"Sunday, Mom. In the meantime, you and Dad can try to figure out new ways to promote Safe Havens."

"Okay. Nina says you're putting in long hours."

"She does too."

"She goes home to Bob. You climb up the attic stairs."

# Five

Roxy was talking on the phone when the doorbell chimed late that afternoon. Louey raced past her office door to answer it. Thanks to Dennis's reading him a story and everyone making a fuss over the boy, he'd shed his timidity.

In seconds she heard his joyful scream. "Mommy! Balloons!"

Roxy quickly got off the phone. She looked in her purse for change to tip the delivery man, then stepped into the hall. Louey barreled by, clutching a bouquet of congratulatory balloons tied with a huge red bow. The balloons flapped in his wake.

"Watch out," Roxy called. "You'll trip."

Maggie ran down the stairs to see what all the commotion was about. Katherine and Allison and their children joined them.

Nina read the envelope attached to the big red bow. "They're for you, Maggie."

"Me?" Maggie cried. "Who would send me balloons?" She took the card out and laughed happily. "They're from Dennis and his secretary, Patricia. They're congratulating me on my new job. I still can't believe it." She turned to Katherine and Allison. "If a miracle can happen to me, it can happen to you too. I literally didn't know where to turn. Then a friend told me about Safe Havens, and now thanks to you, Roxy, I met Dennis Jorden. He's changing my life."

He was changing hers too, Roxy thought. He continually invaded her thoughts. On a moment's notice she could see him in her mind's eye, his wide chest, bulging biceps, rock-hard thighs. But devouring kisses and chemical combustion didn't make sense. Opposites might attract, but they didn't lead to permanence.

As for her own inability to resist his kisses, Roxy attributed it to hormones. After her first disappointingly miserable sexual encounter, it had been easy to maintain a sensible distance from men. She blamed that first disaster on being young and having raging hormones. Hormones that had conveniently lain dormant until Dennis came along.

Exercise! That's what she needed. Parachute jumps every weekend the weather allowed.

Maggie's voice called her back to the present. "Men like Dennis," she was saying, "don't come along often. I should know. Now I'm going to learn to use a computer, earn money, and be independent. I'll be able to care for myself and Louey. How can I ever thank you, Roxy?"

"Please don't," Roxy said. "We're thrilled for you."

"We'll move as soon as we can find a rental."

"There's no hurry." How could she have forgotten to ask Dennis about his interview with Maggie? Roxy wondered. Was it because he kept transporting her to a trembling state of passion in a matter of moments, wiping everything but him from her mind? Maggie's interview was important. She should have remembered.

Louey, holding the balloons tightly in one hand, turned to her. "Dennis promised to read me more stories. He's taking me to the toy store too. He said I can pick any toy I want. I made him a picture. See?"

His face shining with happiness, he thrust the drawing into her hand. Roxy looked at the family picture of three stick figures with circles for heads. They were smiling. He had colored the sky blue and the grass green.

"It's wonderful," she said to him.

"I know." He ran to his mother to show it to her.

Roxy caught Nina's eye and laughed.

As the other two women talked enthusiastically with Maggie, Roxy returned to her office. Beyond the window the sunset flared a brilliant shade of golden amber, reminding her of Dennis's hair. Terrific, she thought. Now she was seeing him in nature! How could she, a grown woman, flutter like an impressionable girl meeting a movie star? She knew better. Rather than dwell on other aspects of his rugged countenance—his clear gray eyes that alternately teased, coaxed, and enticed; or his tempting mouth; or his low rumble of hearty laughter—she fled the office to run downstairs to the cellar. She lost track of time, sorting, washing, drying, and folding four loads of laundry.

On her fifth trip lugging up baskets of clean laundry, Maggie stopped her, grabbing the basket from her hands. "Roxy, you're bushed. I'll fold this. You rest for a little while. You've been on the go all day."

Roxy didn't have to be asked twice. She wanted to be alert for tonight. Heaven forbid if she didn't pay attention to Dennis's new bookkeeping system. Thanking Maggie, she went upstairs to wash, brush her hair, then slip on a pair of clean blue jeans and a yellow scoop-neck sweater. Then she lay down to catch her breath.

She dreamed a warm hand was caressing her face and snuggled closer to it. She purred her appreciation of soft kisses being placed on her cheeks and eyelids. The kisses heated, trailing down her neck to nestle above her breasts, lingering on the bare flesh where her top met her skin. She dreamed strong arms were raising her from the pillow, and a familiar masculine scent wafted through her subconscious.

"Mmmm, nice," she murmured, half-asleep, her eyes still closed.

Dennis had come upstairs to find her asleep. He had stared his fill, fascinated by the even rise and fall of her breasts, and unable to resist sitting down next to her. Even in repose she was a ruby, all fire and flame. He was conscious of his pulsing heartbeat, of his need to join his body with hers. For now, he would settle for her smile when she awoke to see he was the lover of her dreams.

"You like that, do you?" he said huskily. "I'm praying the bed doesn't break. Move over."

Roxy's eyes flew open. Dennis's face, his roguish grin, were a scant inch from hers. She had smelled him in her dream. Welcomed his hands on her. She reared back. "What are you doing here?"

That had thoroughly doused his dream of her dragging him down on the bed, Dennis thought.

"Who were you expecting?" he asked.

"I asked first."

The question was so in keeping with Roxy, he chuckled. "All right. I was kissing you. Now that you're awake, I'd cherish a little cooperation. And speed. I have it on good authority that this bed is programmed with a built-in self-destruct timer."

He handed her a rose and before she could stop him, lowered his face to nuzzle her neck. "You smell good. One of these days I'm going to taste you to my heart's delight. Yours, too, by the way."

Roxy groaned. How would he ever take her seriously if the minute they saw each other, they were either glued horizontally or pasted vertically? The hours of housework she had done to get him out of her mind mocked her useless efforts.

She pushed him away before she gave in to the urge to pull him down. "Don't do that. Get up. You're not supposed to be in my bedroom. Stop giving me presents. It implies a relationship, which we don't have."

He didn't bother hiding his irritation. "You're welcome, grouch. I like you better when you're asleep. Then I don't have to hear your viperish tongue. Don't tell me what to do. I'll give you presents whenever I feel like it. I came up to speak to you in private, which is difficult to do in a house crawling with people. Nina and I introduced ourselves downstairs, and we had a nice chat. She says you're expecting five more people tomorrow. Where do you plan on stashing them? Up on the roof? In the cellar?"

Roxy scrambled off the bed, yanking down her sweater. "We've got it all figured out."

Hunched over, Dennis followed her to the center of the room, where he stood upright. "This is ridiculous."

"You're right. We can't keep doing this."

But he was. His arms were suddenly around her, and she didn't have the desire or the energy to break away. He stared at her for a long time, his eyes darker than usual, more intense. Then his gaze dropped to her breasts, which were crushed against him. She could feel her nipples responding to him, feel her traitorous body yield by inches.

"Why are you being hypocritical?" he asked softly. "Roxy, you're a sensual woman. Why pretend you're not?"

"I . . ." Her voice faltered.

Dennis grew still, hoping she would open up, tell him why she resisted him. "What is it? What aren't you telling me?"

She bit her lip. "Nothing. Nothing except that I have no time for an affair. Especially now. Especially with you."

"Explain that," he said flatly.

Tears filled her eyes. She was afraid to lose her heart, she answered him silently. When he spoke to her in gentle tones and gazed at her with tenderness, she longed to give in to him, allow him to take her away from all of her responsibilities and love her. "I admit you're good-looking and I'm attracted to you."

He dropped his arms. "If that's a compliment, why does it sound like an insult?"

Her face paled. She was going about it all wrong. She wasn't trying to hurt him. It would be different if they had more in common than their explosive desire. They were like two incendiary bombs igniting at once. But desire wasn't love.

"It's not your fault," she said lamely. "It's the way I am."

Fairly steaming with annoyance, Dennis lifted her chin. In her eyes he saw distress mingled with desire. "I'm not your enemy. I would never knowingly hurt you, but I can't prove that if you don't trust me, if you don't see me for who I am. You're so immersed in helping others, you won't help yourself."

She bristled, jerking back from him. "I don't need help. I didn't ask for this. I've got to get back to work."

They stared at each other for a tense moment, during which Dennis silently cursed all the miserable heartbreaking stories she heard daily. He guessed that her skittishness arose partly from that, from the lousy examples of men and marriage she saw through those women. But that couldn't be all of it. There had to be more.

"I don't know what's driving you," he said. "Whatever it is, it isn't driving Nina."

From what she'd told him of the Arnouths, two finer people didn't exist. He suspected both would agree the shelter should be operated differently, more like a business rather than a one-woman attempt to save the world.

"This place isn't large enough," he went on when she didn't respond, "for you to say yes to everyone with a sad story. If you insist on taking in more people than you can handle, why can't Nina take some into her home?"

"I wouldn't ask her," she said immediately. "Safe Havens started here. If we can move to larger quarters, maybe things will change. I'm not trying to be a martyr, believe me. It's just the way things are. You can't pigeonhole people's problems into neat time slots."

"You're not running a hospital or a prison. You aren't a nurse or a keeper. Shut off the phone at night. Let the answering machine take the calls. Why should everyone else sleep in a comfortable bed, walk down a hall if they need to use a bathroom, and not you? You yourself told me you wished you could spend an uninterrupted hour in a bathtub. When the hell do you relax?"

She scowled at him. "Stop making it sound as if I don't. You forget we met when I had taken the afternoon off to relax. I skydive."

"That's death-defying, not relaxing."

"Lower your voice. There are people downstairs."

He stared at her, his gaze touching her lips, then sweeping over her body before returning to her eyes. Roxy didn't have the pale skin of a redhead. She had a rosy tint to her flesh that deepened whenever she was nervous, as she was now. "Roxy, come home with me this weekend."

Roxy's heart thundered. She felt her face flush as passion sparkled within her. Her breath caught in her throat, visions of spending the night with him almost irresistible. Still, she resisted, turning away. "I can't."

"You mean you won't." He grabbed her arms, forcing her to face him again. He couldn't keep the bitterness and disappointment from his voice. "How can this be enough for you?"

"Dennis, we're not suited. If you would stop to think clearly, you would know that too. I'm disorganized and have a touchy temper. I'm committed to my work. I jump out of airplanes. Math bores me. I bet you've never marched in a parade for a social cause."

"No, but what's that supposed to prove?"

"It indicates—no, it shows—I'm right."

His hands swept over her shoulders to her back, gliding downward to cup her buttocks. "What about need? The need between a man and a woman. Your need and mine." He brought her forward. "This proves we're very suited. Kiss me, Roxy. Prove you're right."

She uttered a little gasp as she felt the hard evidence of his need. As if of their own accord, her hands slid up his arms and over his broad shoulders. Too many things threatened to slip from her control if she wasn't steadfast, yet she didn't want him angry with her. "What harm can there be," she murmured, "if I give you a thank-you kiss for what you did for Maggie?"

He dropped the lightest of kisses on her lips. She barely felt it. When she tried to apply pressure, he put his hands on her shoulders, keeping the contact coolly casual. "Why must you give yourself an excuse when you know you want to kiss me?" He ran his knuckles under her jaw. "You schedule every hour of your day on your bulletin board. Everyone knows where to find you and rush at you all day and night. Skydiving may be fun for you, but it's a solo act. When do you include others? Or is maintaining this life-style exactly what you want so you don't have to take risks?"

"What are you talking about?" she demanded.

"This." Her breath quickened as his body molded itself to hers, tucking her between his muscular legs. "I dare you to kiss me the way you're dying to. With no excuses."

"That's childish."

"Bull! You're scared. You're petrified you might feel too much."

"No!"

"Prove it. I dare you to let your feelings go."

She was aware of his masculine scent, his compelling voice. His anger. And his desire, for her. In a quick movement, before she let herself think of the ramifications, she grasped his head and brought it down to hers. She tried to obliterate each challenging truth by thrusting her tongue into his mouth, proving him wrong. Her fingers curled in his hair.

His hand lifted the hem of her sweater and slipped beneath to massage her breast. Her breathing quickened, and he gave a grunt of satisfaction.

Dennis took over the kiss, elevating it from a mating of two mouths to a sensory world. The simple attic, with its sparse furnishings, could have been the finest hotel suite. Roxy wouldn't have cared, though. Quivering from the intensity of her emotions, she cared only about discovery. His lips on hers were all that mattered. Her body pressed to his was her only reality.

His tongue invaded her mouth, demanding a response. As before, she yielded automatically, returning his kiss with ardent fervor. When he finally released her, she was dazed and weak, and his eyes were blazing fiercely. She could feel his throbbing heat, even through his clothes. Each stared at the other, stunned anew by their tempestuous reactions.

"Change your mind, Roxy," Dennis whispered. "Spend the weekend with me. Don't cheat us. People work. People play. People love. It's obvious we can't be in the same room without wanting each other. Let me show you you have nothing to fear."

Except losing her heart. She put her hand on his chest. "I'm going to my parents' Sunday."

He cradled her face between his palms and bent his head to brush his lips over hers. "That leaves Friday night, Saturday, and Saturday night. Roxy, I want to make love with you, to caress you and cherish you. Without an audience, on a bed that won't crash-land. I want to hear you sigh my name in pleasure as we kiss good night. I want you to wake me up in the middle of the night seeking a repeat of what we give to each other. I want you to need me inside you, as I need to be part of you."

On fire from the visions his words painted, she shivered as he stroked her hair. Her breasts ached for his touch. The lightweight sweater she wore suddenly constricted her, as if it were a heavy plaster cast. On a deeply feminine level she yearned to say yes.

"Is it wrong to want?" he asked. His lips grazed her temple.

"It is for me," she said, fighting to sweep away the evocative pictures he painted. "I told you Nina and Bob are hoping to have a baby. If she isn't already pregnant, she could be soon. She conceives easily. It's carrying to term that's difficult for her. You saw Maggie's state of mind before you rescued her. Multiply her desperation by every woman who comes through my door, seeking help, and you'll have a small idea of what Nina and I face daily, and what I will shoulder alone. They need me. This is my life. I can't turn my back on it."

"Am I asking you to turn your back on Safe Havens?" he demanded, his sexual need firing his temper. "This has nothing to do with Nina's hypothetical pregnancy, or the women you help. I'll tell you what surprises me most, Roxy. You spend your life telling women to face the truth about the forces that brought them to where they are today, yet you lie to yourself."

Her mouth went dry, and her stomach muscles tightened. She sensed he could see into her soul, that he knew the real reason she resisted was out of Fear. The fear that like the women she helped, she would not only give Dennis her body, but also her heart and all that she was, thereby risking losing everything.

At her sister's funeral she had made a sacred pledge. She hadn't been able to help Alice, but she'd vowed to help as many other women like her as she could. By devoting her energies to Safe Havens, she kept that pledge. How could she help others if those energies were taken up by a torrid affair?

She stared at Dennis, unable to answer his charge. Thankfully, she didn't have to. Nina shouted up the stairs that Bob had arrived.

"We have to go down," Roxy said, and quickly turned away.

Using an excuse to put on a pot of coffee, she escaped while Dennis joined the Arnouths in the office. First she fled to the bathroom, locked the door, and looked in the mirror. She quickly brushed her wild hair, then pressed a cold wet cloth to her swollen lips.

"Darn you, Dennis Jorden. We aren't suited. Darn you for coming into my life and mixing me up!"

When she entered the office carrying a tray laden with cups, a pot of coffee, and a plate of cookies, Dennis took the tray from her and set it down on the desk. He noticed the warm flush on her face, the way she avoided meeting his eyes.

"Roxy," Bob said, drawing both their attentions. "Dennis and I have discovered we know many of the same people."

"I think it's terrific," Nina said. "Dennis, we're having a dinner party Saturday night. Will you come? Roxy can show you the way."

"Thank you. I'd like that," he said, turning to Roxy.

She didn't look at him. She knew that if she

went with him, it would be more than a date. She would be giving tacit agreement to deepen their relationship. She was acutely aware that all eyes had focused on her. With a hollow feeling in the pit of her stomach, she declined. "I'm sorry. I'm going away for the weekend. I'm leaving Saturday for my folks'."

Dennis's jaw tightened. It was the only sign he gave that he knew he was the reason for her refusal. He drank his coffee, then in a calm, implacable voice, he discussed recent changes in the tax laws as they pertained to charities in general, Safe Havens in particular. In concise, efficient, businesslike terms he brought them up-to-date, then explained his record-keeping system.

Roxy shook with nerves. Throughout his talk she sat in miserable isolation, acutely aware of the tension in the room, the unhappiness, which was her fault. The good cheer had fizzled, replaced by Nina's censure and Dennis's displeasure. Gone was the teasing glint in his eye, the humor that lightened his voice. He was a stranger.

She was right to refuse, she told herself. She had no doubt they could spin planets out of their orbits if they made love, but they were wrong for each other.

"Roxy, do you have any questions before I leave?"

"What?" She nearly jumped.

"I asked," Dennis said, "if you understood."

Her control slipped. She hadn't heard a word he'd said. She could tell him to begin again, admit she hadn't paid attention to his discussion of numbers, columns, and state and federal law. It would prove her point that she couldn't mix business with pleasure.

"No," she said instead. "I understand perfectly. Thank you for coming." The price of independence, of sticking to one's goal, she realized dully, was towering resentment.

Nina's gaze shifted from Roxy's bleak expression to Dennis's granite features. "Dennis, feel free to bring a guest Saturday night."

"Thanks, I will. Roxy, walk me out." At the front door he shoved his hands into his pockets and faced her. "I'm going to ask Maggie to go with me Saturday. Since you're the housemother here, I thought you should know."

Roxy drew in a sharp breath. She felt as if a rock had landed in her stomach. How he had fooled her with his charm! His gentle urging! She was right not to trust him.

His silky voice went on, and she was held captive by his mocking tone and the words that cut her like a knife. "You didn't have to lie about why you couldn't go. But don't worry, you won't need your protective barrier to keep me away anymore. I got your message loud and clear. You're on your own now."

The color drained from her cheeks as, without another word, he left. She flew back into the den. "What do you think you're doing?" she demanded of Nina.

Nina glanced at her. "Putting dirty dishes on the tray."

"You know I'm talking about Dennis. How could you invite him to bring a date? What possessed you?"

"Bob, hand me that cup, please. Aren't you overreacting, Roxy? Why should you care if I prefer an even number of people at my dinner table?"

"You're dense, Nina. Dense! He's going to ask Maggie."

Nina checked the room for any missed dishes. "I like Maggie."

Roxy's hands flew to her hips. "Is that all you have to say? You like her?"

"What more should I say? You don't want him. You've made that clear to him, and right in front of us, I might add. Why be angry at him if you're the one who rejected him? If he doesn't ask Maggie, I'm sure there are plenty of women who would jump at the chance to be his date. He's dashing, intelligent, has a warm sense of humor, and even you said he's handsome. Just your type— physically. Maggie could do worse. Give your parents my regards Saturday night. I'm glad you're finally taking a weekend off, now that you've worked everything out your way."

Roxy threw herself into a chair. She had only herself to thank, she realized. Nina was right. She had got her wish. She would have all the time in the world to devote to Safe Havens, because Dennis wouldn't bother her in the future. She had seen to that.

She had thrown him into Maggie's arms.

After she'd finished cleaning up, Nina gathered her purse and jacket. "I'll see you in the morning, Roxy. Maybe by then you'll come to your senses and phone Dennis. He hasn't asked her yet. But he will see Maggie at work. Besides, your parents don't expect you until Sunday."

"Nina means well," Bob said after his wife had left the office. "She wants to see you happy. I do too. We worry about you."

Roxy looked up at him. Bob was a kindly-looking man with thinning brown hair and hazel eyes. But his cherubic face masked a razor-sharp mind. She displayed her independent streak for his benefit. "I'll be fine if people stop trying to run my life."

Behind his glasses Bob's eyes were warm with concern. "Then you should be thrilled Nina suggested Dennis bring a date. Incidentally, you didn't hear a word he said when he explained the record-keeping system, did you?"

She smiled wryly. "So shoot me."

After the Arnouths left, Roxy locked up the house and climbed the stairs to the attic. She got out her sleeping bag to give it an airing before she let Shannon use her room.

She glanced dispiritedly at the bed where Dennis had fused their bodies in a fierce embrace. Recalling her wanton response to his ravishing kisses, she felt her heart quicken, her cheeks burn. Dennis had perfected all the right moves. One touch, and wham! Physical and emotional fireworks. Guaranteed to last as long as she fell for his favorite word—fate. When "fate" failed, he blithely switched women.

Thank goodness, Roxy thought, she had resisted total temptation. Correction. In all honesty, only the broken bed had refused carnal completion. A few more enticing minutes in her earlier dreamlike state, and who knows what she might have agreed to. One thing about Dennis she could appreciate. He led, he didn't demand. He seduced with soft words and let her paint erotic pictures. After stimulating a lady, he let her make up her mind. Who could fault his technique? Statistics guaranteed success.

But not with her.

• • •

Irked at Roxy's ability to slam the door on what was clearly happening between them, Dennis drove home stewing. Roxy feared getting involved with him, but there was no involvement. How could there be? Her bed stopped him from making love to her, and she said she didn't have room in her life for him. *Especially him.*

He shot past a car, then spied a patrol car and trimmed his speed, staying within the speed limit. How could she think making love with him would splinter her precious time and energy? Foolish woman. Why couldn't she see she could have both?

He pulled up to a red light. The residents of Safe Havens didn't need Roxy for a keeper. They tidied up after themselves and their children. They shared cooking chores. All they needed from Roxy was a temporary shelter, counseling, legal advice, protection, a job. And permanent housing.

The light switched to green. The patrol car was directly behind him, and Dennis drove cautiously.

Caution. Roxy's middle name. What made her so infuriatingly cautious? Considering what they did to each other physically, considering she was the most responsive woman he'd ever held in his arms, he couldn't figure her out. He had felt her body's response. She could be tender and funny and vibrantly alive. How could she turn off the sizzling sexual current?

He pulled into his driveway. The porch light shone a welcome. He had wanted Roxy to see his home. The fifty-five-year-old house had high ceilings, detailed carved moldings, oak floors. He even had a special surprise for her. Now she wouldn't enjoy it.

He wasn't tired, so he switched on the lights in his office where he kept his Compaq computer. He tossed his jacket onto a black leather chair, loosened his tie, and turned on the computer, bringing up the fraud case he was working on for his writer client in California. The man had signed a contract to write a movie script, negotiating a net-profit deal. After the movie was released, he was told there were no profits, although the movie had earned millions. The profits were structured into the costs to hide more millions, all under the guise of expenses. The amount in question would be enough for Roxy to run Safe Havens forever.

Roxy. He wanted her. She wanted him. It galled him that she felt safer jumping out of airplanes than risking a chance with her heart. What was worse than a one-sided love affair that went nowhere? Nothing. Disgusted, he switched off the computer.

Upstairs, he stripped, showered, and slipped naked into his king-size bed. Above, a canopy of skylights allowed heavenly viewing at the touch of the button that controlled the retractable ceiling. The spacious master suite, converted to its size by combining two rooms, allowed the eye to flow from the sleeping to the sitting area, and beyond to a secluded redwood deck.

Tonight, though, Dennis's mind was on an elusive fiery comet named Roxy. A half hour later he closed the ceiling, turned over on his side, and fell asleep cursing fate.

# *Six*

After a restless night Roxy awoke to face an
indisputable fact: Her exhaustion and frazzled
nerves stemmed from more than simple fatigue.
Dennis was the cause. Two weeks ago she hadn't
known he existed. Now she couldn't dislodge him
from her mind. He evoked a passionate, dissolving
awareness in her. And he knew it. Counted on it.
Which was why her refusal the night before had
taken him by surprise, sounding heartless and
insensitive before an audience. She hadn't meant
to hurt him. She had simply listened to her
common-sense inner voice caution her against
leading with her heart.

As Nina said, why should she care who Dennis
dated? She didn't. Nor did she care how he spent
his private time. Or with whom. Except in the case
of Maggie. A date with Dennis was the last thing
she needed in her vulnerable state. Maggie first
had to understand and deal with the forces that
had driven her life to its present tenuous state.
She had to rebuild her self-worth. Maggie was in a
fragile state. She could grow strong and indepen-

dent, rebuild her self-confidence, or she could disintegrate emotionally, crushed by stresses beyond her control.

Roxy had to see Dennis. Not that she wanted to, of course, but she felt a duty to Maggie since she, Roxy, was the one who had introduced them. Dennis must understand she was not providing a dating service at Safe Havens. She'd swallow her pride and convince him to ask someone else to Nina's party, rather than risk setting Maggie back.

Dennis was simply too charming. She knew that for a fact. No other man had ever been so adept at testing her resolve. One touch sent her to the stratosphere.

The room suddenly became oppressive with memories. As she got up, she resisted looking back at the bed, where Dennis had given her more physical delight than she'd ever known. If only, a tiny voice inside of her said, she weren't so afraid of losing herself to him.

Roxy immediately discounted the little voice. She wasn't afraid, she was cautious. And smart.

She slipped her robe on over her shortie night-gown, then peered out the window at the cloudy sky. Her father claimed looking out the window was as good, if not better, than listening to a bunch of weather forecasters make wrong predictions. She could imagine Dennis agreeing with her father.

Her father would like Dennis. He, too, disapproved of her jumping out of planes. Her mother would definitely like Dennis, but then again, she wanted to see Roxy married. Her mom praised her for being sensible, for making good choices. Therefore, it stood to reason her mother would assume Roxy knew everything there was to know about Dennis, and she would welcome him with

open arms. One look at his golden hair, his twin-
kling grey eyes, his dynamite physique, and she
would conclude that any child of Dennis and her
daughter's would be beautiful.

She would probably be right.

Roxy passed a critical eye over the room. The
house had not been designed to be used as a
multiple-family dwelling. She tried not to be-
grudge the women and children who needed her
their more comfortable quarters and easy access
to a bathroom, while she was stuck in the small
attic room. Yet ever since Dennis had told her that
she had to take care of herself, too, she was
remembering the pleasures of having her home to
herself and the opportunity for hourlong soaks in
the tub. And to sleep the night through! Last
night, again, she'd received an emergency call
around 3:00 A.M.

Not that Roxy would ever give up Safe Havens,
but were Dennis and Nina and Bob and her
parents maybe a little right?

She climbed down the attic stairs and luckily
found the bathroom empty. Eyeing the claw-
footed bathtub, she promised herself that one of
these days she would hang a DO NOT DISTURB sign
on the door and treat herself to the luxury of a
scented bath. This morning, though, she showered quickly, then put her nightgown and robe
back on before heading downstairs for a cup of
coffee. When she reached the downstairs hallway,
her hair still tousled and damp from the shower,
she stopped short. Dennis was the last man she
expected to see in her house! Her mouth dropped
open, her eyes widened, her heart leaped into her
throat.

He looked absurdly handsome in a dark gray
suit. His arms were laden with a laptop computer

and a box of operating manuals. Louey was at his side, carrying his newest drawing. His face was wreathed in smiles, smiles he showered first on Dennis, then on her.

The boy showed her his new cowboy buckle. "Dennis gave me this. It's neat. As soon as Dennis brings this to Mommy's room, we're going to breakfast. Hurry up and get dressed, Roxy. You come too."

Dennis greeted her with a perfunctory good morning. "I'm driving Maggie to work," he explained.

Maggie raced down the stairs at that moment. Roxy was amazed at her transformation. She looked radiant in a blue suit and white blouse, with tiny blue earrings in her lobes. She again wore heavy makeup to cover her bruises, and her doelike eyes shone with happiness. And like her son, she aimed her shower of joy on the man responsible for it.

Dennis.

Roxy complimented Maggie on her appearance, and Dennis echoed her. Then he asked Maggie where she wanted the computer and the books.

Maggie shyly requested he put them in her bedroom. Dennis nodded and went upstairs.

Roxy stayed rooted to the floor.

Louey tugged at her hand. "Come on, Roxy. Don't you want to go with us? I like you."

"I like you, too, but I can't go. I'm not dressed."

Louey shook his head. "No. We're having a party." He appealed to Dennis when he returned. "You want Roxy to come, right?"

Over the boy's head Dennis shot Roxy a look that could freeze the whole of Lake Erie. On her part, her hands were balled into fists at her sides. Dennis had the perfect opportunity to pay her back for her treatment of him in front of the Arnouths the previous night.

He looked down at Louey, then back up at Roxy. His hard gaze seemed to strip her of her clothes, seeing past her defenses and right into her soul. His lips thinned, and she guessed he didn't like what he saw.

"I'll wait in the car," he said. "Don't be long."

Louey had trapped them both. Roxy raced upstairs, changed into a soft yellow dress that fell gently away from her hips, grabbed a jacket, and was outside in ten minutes. Maggie and Louey sat in the rear seat of Dennis's car. No sooner had she closed her door than he roared down the street.

Louey kept up a constant chatter while Roxy couldn't help recalling the last time she'd been in Dennis's car. They'd necked in the backseat! Her gaze slid to his strong profile, then flicked away. He kept his eyes straight ahead as he whipped through early-morning traffic.

He parked in front of a diner. "We'll get faster service here."

"I like this place," Louey said as the hostess showed them to a booth. He slid onto the bench next to his mother, leaving Dennis and Roxy to sit together on the opposite bench.

Dennis flipped open the menu as soon as he sat down. His thigh pressed against hers in the narrow booth.

Roxy held up her menu, pretending to study it. If she ate, though, she'd probably get sick.

Dennis ordered bacon and eggs over easy, a short stack, and coffee.

Roxy ordered plain yogurt, hoping the enzymes in it would calm her upset stomach. She marveled at Dennis's restorative abilities. After his supposed great hurt of the previous night, he not only had a new female interest but a fabulous appetite.

During the meal he didn't say a word to Roxy, except to ask her for the salt and pepper. He directed all his remarks to Louey and Maggie, until Roxy felt like a third wheel. Or a chaperon.

"I have to go to the bathroom," Louey said halfway through the meal.

Maggie excused herself and Louey from the table.

Roxy was sitting so close to Dennis she could feel his heat. As unnerving—and arousing—as that was, she had to warn him that he'd be playing with fire if he asked Maggie to Nina's party. But how could she say it without getting him angry?

"Dennis," she began, "I didn't want to come here, but since I am here, we have to talk."

He put down his fork and turned to face her. "If Maggie hadn't needed the computer and the books, I would have waited for her outside. I don't make a practice of being where I'm not wanted. As for talking, there's nothing to say. You said it all last night. I'm not happy you're here. As soon as we're done eating, I'm taking you back to Safe Havens." His voice was low, yet it echoed like thunder.

For an endless moment they sat gazing at each other, emotions simmering on the surface. He was staring at her with an expression she would never forget. Repudiation. Preferring the warm, teasing glint in his eyes to this dismissal, Roxy was saddened by the change in him. The change she herself had caused.

Louey scampered back to the table, followed by Maggie, thus preventing Roxy from speaking. Her opportunity to convince Dennis he shouldn't date Maggie had passed.

"I'm so lucky," Maggie said. "You two are the

nicest couple I've ever known. I don't think there's a cruel thought that passes your minds."

Roxy reached for her glass of water.

"Thanks for saying we're nice people," Dennis said, eliminating the word "couple." "But this nice man and his new nice secretary have to go to work. So finish up, everybody."

Roxy had the beginnings of a headache.

Dennis said only a cursory good-bye when he dropped her and Louey off at her house. Maggie waved cheerfully as she slid into the front seat next to Dennis. Roxy plastered a smile on her face and waved back.

She stormed into the house. From a rough beginning her day worsened. Everything that could go wrong did. She filled out the wrong government forms for several women and had to repeat the tedious task. She spent an hour searching for a file, only to find it on her desk hiding under another folder. Forgetting that she was making tea, she scorched a new enamel pot. At last she escaped from the house to shop for groceries. As soon as she got home, though, she dropped the bag containing a sack of flour and a carton of eggs on the kitchen floor. The flour split open to liberally dust the floor and coat the dozen splattered eggs.

Nina found her on her hands and knees in the kitchen, cleaning. Afternoon sun had replaced the morning clouds. It spilled through the windows onto the linoleum floor, highlighting the gloppy mess.

Nina shook her head as Roxy told her everything that had gone wrong that day, including her not talking to Dennis about Maggie.

"What will you do?" Nina asked.

Roxy brushed back her hair. "If you mean will I

give up, the answer is no. I can't. Maggie is in a tenuous emotional state. You don't think Dennis should date her, do you?"

Nina smothered a laugh. "No, I don't," she said solemnly. "You're wise to think of her. And Louey."

Roxy squeezed the water from the mop, nodding in agreement.

"How many calls last night?" Nina asked.

"Only one."

"I still say you should turn on the answering machine. I wish you'd realize there's nothing you can do in the middle of the night that can't wait until morning." She went on to say that a friend at the county crisis center had located a psychologist to lead the group counseling sessions for the coming week.

Roxy was glad the subject had shifted away from Dennis and onto more important matters. When the doorbell rang, she assumed it was Shannon O'Brien. It was.

Shannon was in her late thirties, a slightly built woman with dark hair and blue eyes. She was carrying an infant and looked as if she could use a hot meal and twenty-four hours of sleep. Her three other children, two boys and a girl, stood silently at her side. None looked glad to be there. Roxy couldn't blame them. They were shell-shocked from losing their father, their home, and all their belongings.

"Come in." Roxy stepped aside. "We can talk over lunch. How old is the baby?"

The oldest boy introduced himself as John. "I'm twelve. Ellie is three months. Felicity is nine. Aaron is four. Thank you for taking us in. I can tell you what happened. My mother is tired."

Roxy liked the youth, who was assuming the role of head of the family. "Thank you, John."

Nina and Roxy whipped up a batch of sandwiches. John ate quickly, telling them that an electrical fire had destroyed their house.

"We had a business in our home," Shannon added. "I started it when my husband took ill. The children helped after school."

Louey zipped into the kitchen just then, and Roxy introduced him. Then she suggested he invite Aaron and Felicity into the den to watch television with him. The three raced off, leaving Shannon, John, and the baby.

In answer to Nina's question, Shannon said she made Christmas wreaths and bows, window shades to keep out drafts, and clown dolls. The children helped by attaching felt cutouts on Styrofoam balls to create the clowns' faces. They sold their work through catalogs and on consignment.

"John was in charge of the packaging and the mailing," she went on. "He worked on weekends and after school. It's all gone now. Burned. My sewing machine, materials, everything." She wiped her eyes. "Even our mailing lists are gone." She shook her head.

"What about your husband's life insurance and your homeowner's insurance?" Roxy asked. "Have you filed a claim? Has the insurance adjuster told you when to expect your check?"

"We're having trouble. My husband was ill for a long time, and the life-insurance company claims we didn't fill out the forms properly. They're piling on red tape to exhaust me. Normally, I can deal with it, but now I feel overwhelmed."

Nina and Roxy said they understood, then Nina turned to Roxy. "Why not ask Dennis for help?"

she suggested. "He knows how to deal with red tape and regulations."

Roxy nodded. Whatever was between them, she believed that if Dennis knew about Shannon's dire straits, he would help. Excusing herself, she went to her office to call. Her hand shook as she dialed his work number. The phone rang twice, before Maggie answered.

"Roxy! How nice. Dennis will be so pleased to hear from you."

Roxy doubted that. Maggie put her on hold, then came back on the line less than a minute later. "Roxy, I'm sorry. Dennis is busy. He wants to know why you're calling."

"Please tell him it's business." She kept her tone of voice light for Maggie's sake.

She held on for what seemed an interminable length of time, then Maggie delivered the next message, sounding less cheerful, less bubbly. "Dennis said he explained everything to you last night. If you're still having trouble understanding the bookkeeping system, he said to use the envelopes."

Roxy nearly slammed the receiver down. With effort she kept her voice calm. "Please tell Dennis my business is personal. I didn't want to mention it at breakfast because I knew he was anxious to get to work."

More time out. Roxy paced her office, holding on to the receiver.

Roxy." Maggie sounded flustered and confused. "Dennis says he can't come to the phone now."

*You mean he won't*, Roxy thought. "All right, Maggie. Would you tell him I'll call back later?"

"He's getting ready for a meeting," Maggie said when Roxy phoned half an hour later. "Oh, Roxy, Dennis is wonderful. He's so considerate."

As long as your name isn't Roxy, she thought balefully. "You deserve consideration, Maggie. Give Dennis a message, please."

"Shoot."

*What a great idea,* Roxy thought. But she restrained herself and only said, "Tell him I'll touch base with him later, Maggie."

"Well?" Nina asked when Roxy stormed out of the office.

"I'll kill him," Roxy fumed. "He's doing this deliberately, but I'm not giving up. The women depend on me."

Even Dennis couldn't keep up the charade without Maggie catching on. Two calls later, he agreed to speak to her. Before she could say a word, though, he lit into her, his tone chilly, brusque.

"This is Maggie's first day on the job. She doesn't need you upsetting her."

Roxy ground her teeth to control her temper. She had been right to stop seeing him. She'd thought he was nice, but he was awful. Awful. Defiantly, she told him that.

"Me?" he said icily. "Breakfast was bad enough, but I had no choice. However, I am not the one calling my office, interrupting my busy day. You are."

"I'm not the one delivering messages through Maggie. You are. If you had the decency to accept my call without putting me through this nonsense, I wouldn't be upsetting Maggie."

"Oh, for goodness' sakes! What do you want?"

Roxy took a breath, swallowed her pride, and tried to modulate her voice. "I told you, I need to talk to you."

"And I told you I'm not interested. You said everything you had to say to me last night. With an audience. I'm through being the world's prize chump, Roxy. If you're having trouble with the new record-keeping system, junk it or let Bob do it. Or go back to your envelopes."

She knew he had just cause to be angry with her. Not a half hour before openly rejecting him, she had melted in his arms, returning his kisses and mating her tongue with his, responding in the most elemental way to the contact of his body on hers. He had been aroused, and she had rubbed against him like a cat in heat. Then she'd done her abrupt about-face, hurting a proud and gentle man who had never done anything to her except make her feel more alive than she'd ever felt before.

"Please, Dennis. It's not that. I'm sure your system is wonderful."

"A system isn't wonderful," he snapped. "It's not a person with feelings. It's a tool. An expedient tool. You discard it when you no longer have use of it."

He wasn't talking about a system, he was referring to her callous treatment of him. He was goading her, itching for a fight.

"It's important, Dennis, or I wouldn't keep calling."

He made a disgruntled noise. "You have two minutes. The clock is ticking."

"Not on the phone," she said, carefully trying to reestablish a thread of peace. "I'd rather explain in person."

"You mean as in face-to-face?"

"Yes. Can you come to my home tonight? Say, sevenish?"

"No. Unlike you, I enjoy my evenings. Unlike you, I'm not a workaholic. I've got a date. If you insist on seeing me in person, you come to me."

Her stomach clenched. "All right. I'll meet you at your office."

"No, not here. I have clients coming."

Roxy counted to ten. "Where, then?"

The line crackled with tension, then he said, "My home."

"Your home?"

"That's right. I'm not the one asking, you are. You're free to change your mind. You're good at that."

She was almost too upset to ask, but she forced herself to remember why she had called him. "What time?"

"Say midnightish."

She held the receiver away from her ear, glaring at it. No grass grew under Dennis's feet. He expected her to drive to his house after he'd had a date and no doubt made love to another woman!

"Yes or no?" he asked. "My time's valuable."

She realized he was hoping she'd refuse. And she wanted to, but her duty to Maggie and Shannon was her foremost consideration.

"What's your address?" she asked.

"I'm in the book."

"You're rotten!" she shouted in a flash of fury.

"Tough!"

The line went dead.

Storming into the kitchen, Roxy flung the newspaper off a chair and sat down.

"How did you make out?" Nina asked.

She snorted. "He's mad. Mad."

"As in crazy? Or as in angry?"

"Both! He's childish. He wouldn't take the time to give me his address but told me to look it up in the phone book. You call that the act of a grownup?"

"I call that the act of a man who's hurting. Look

at it from his angle, Roxy. Last night you cut him dead. You told me he asked what you were doing this weekend, so he knew you were free Saturday night. You don't have to tell me what you two were doing up in your room before you came downstairs. It was written on both your faces. You went all mushy when you looked at each other. Frankly, I'm surprised he consented to see you at all tonight."

Roxy crumbled as Nina's accusation struck her to the core. She hadn't wanted to hurt Dennis. She'd been protecting herself, her heart. Now he loathed her, and she couldn't blame him.

Nina handed her the phone book. She flipped through it, found Dennis's address, and wrote it down.

Dennis's blood stirred hotly as he hung up the phone. He was sick and tired of Roxy's damn conditions. Why had she suddenly decided she had to see him? In person yet. Seeing her nearly naked that morning in that froth of a nightgown and robe had been bad enough. And breakfast had been worse. Everytime he'd moved, his thigh had touched hers. Out of aggravation he had purposely set stupid stipulations for her seeing him. Her acceptance amazed him.

He laughed shortly. At least he'd finally found a way to make her answering machine handle latenight calls. Still, he was furious with himself for agreeing to see her.

He forced his irate thoughts from his mind after bluntly informing Pat that if Roxy Harris called again, he was out for the day. "Don't let Maggie hear you, though."

"I thought you liked Roxy. Maggie told me what a good time all of you had at breakfast."

He glowered at her. To think he had wanted to protect Roxy, show her tenderness and understanding. "I did not have a good time. Close the door. I have work to do."

That night Dennis met Steven Ostner at an Italian restaurant for dinner. He knew the maître d' and owner, Charles Marino, well, as did Steven. As they sat down, Steven asked when he was going to meet Dennis's skydiver.

Dennis cursed himself for opening his big mouth and didn't answer.

Throughout dinner, all of Steven's conversation was met with brooding silence from Dennis. The publisher, who was a pro at getting people to open up, leaned back in his chair and assessed his mute dinner companion. In the years he'd known Dennis, he'd known him to be a hardworking, forthright man of impeccable integrity, who always weighed both sides of an issue fairly. He almost always maintained a cheerful demeanor too. Whatever was eating him this night involved a woman. And Steven could guess her name. When he'd informed Dennis that his feature editor had agreed to do an article on Roxy for the Sunday supplement, Dennis had changed the subject. When he'd reported his staff had run a check on Safe Havens and that Roxy and her partner enjoyed excellent reputations, Dennis had signaled the waiter to refill his drink. When he'd said his wife was eager to meet Roxy, Dennis had told him she should call Roxy direct. When he lit a cigarette, Dennis asked for one.

Finally, when they were through dinner, Steven decided to find out what was wrong.

"Okay, Dennis what gives?" he asked. "You

snapped at everyone here tonight, including me. You're not fit to be in human company. You hardly touched your food. And I thought you'd be pleased about the article on Roxy and Safe Havens."

"Why would you think that?" Dennis asked curtly.

"Aren't you the man who said fate brought you two together?"

Dennis threw down his linen napkin. "Only a fool believes in fate. I'm through being a fool."

"I can see how your new belief is making you happy," Steven said wryly. "So happy, it's tearing away at your gut."

"I'll get over it."

"Dennis, you're one of the truly nice guys I know. At least you were. If you and Roxy are having a problem, my advice is to settle it."

Dennis gritted his teeth. Steven had unwittingly touched a raw nerve. As infuriated as he was with Roxy, he felt absurdly cheated that they'd never made love. He couldn't carry a memory of sharing that stunning, radiating ecstasy with her. She had cheated him just as she cheated herself. All she thought about was work and jumping out of airplanes.

"We are not having a problem." He drummed his fingers on the table. "We are not having anything. We're finished."

Steven's eyebrows shot up. "So that's it. You and Roxy had more than a spat."

"We're finished," Dennis repeated.

"Okay. For argument's sake, I'm going to assume it's your fault."

"Mine!" A couple seated nearby looked up. He glared at them. "You know nothing about this, Steven. I'm better off without her. Roxy is brave for others. She'll carry anyone else's standard. But who needs a woman who's afraid to trust her feelings? Where do you come off blaming me?"

"What I mean," Steven said in a conciliatory tone, "is that if Roxy means as much to you as I suspect, I don't think you should give up without a fight. You'll have the rest of your life to regret it if you do."

"The only thing I regret is wasting my new secretary's time with needless calls. That's another thing I have to thank Roxy for."

"My, my." Steven chuckled. "Things really heated up fast between you two, didn't they? Since you're the great proponent of fate, why not give fate another chance? Who knows? She might have great things in store for you."

Still filled with hot, scorching resentment that he'd let himself be played for a fool, Dennis muttered a curse under his breath. He was an idiot. A damned fool idiot! What else could you call a man who got aroused just hearing a woman's voice on the phone? A stab of desire teased his brain. But just as swiftly as it emerged, he squelched it.

"Don't spout platitudes at me, Steven. For a smart man, you don't make sense."

"Maybe so, but I'm happily married to Antonia, who as you know is a spunky redhead. Like your Roxy."

"She is not my Roxy!"

"It wasn't all smooth sailing in the beginning for Tonia and me," Steven went on, becoming serious. "There were . . . certain problems we had to learn to overcome. We communicate. Intimately and otherwise. The best part of loving her is knowing it's going to continue.

"So you tell me—if I'm not smart, what are you?"

Dennis tossed back the last of his drink. "Lucky!"

# *Seven*

For once, keeping busy didn't help Roxy. Dennis had made it clear he didn't want to see her anymore than she wanted to see him. By the time Nina was ready to leave for the day, Roxy had a serious case of cold feet. She tried to convince Nina to talk to Dennis instead.

"It doesn't matter which one of us speaks with him, Nina. And he'll be more amenable if you make the request."

Nina flatly refused. "No. In the first place I will not tell him who he can and can't bring to my house. In the second place I've got an appointment in a few minutes. In the third place the only man I date at midnight is Bob. This was your idea. You made the arrangements, you see it through."

By eleven that night Roxy's temper was hitting a boiling point. While Dennis was out on a date charming some woman, she was watching the time tick by.

*Midnightish!* She had news for Dennis. Midnightish in her book was going to be twelve-thirty. Or later.

For her appointment she took extra time with her makeup and brushed her hair until it shone. She wore a below-the-knee denim skirt and a peach cotton blouse. If she wore one of her nice dresses, Dennis would think she was trying to come on to him.

At thirty-five minutes past twelve, Roxy switched on the answering machine. Every bed was filled, including hers, where Shannon slept with Felicity. The baby was in the crib next to the bed. John and Aaron slept on cots downstairs.

Roxy backed her car out of the driveway. Preoccupied, she banged into the curb. Normally, she found driving relaxing, since it gave her time to be alone. Not tonight, though. Muttering a curse, she set the car on the road and took off. How dare Dennis drag her out of her house at such an ungodly hour? She was sorely tempted to check into a motel, take the phone off the hook, and soak in a tub while Dennis waited up for her!

A full moon lit up the starry sky. She knew the quiet residential area Dennis lived in and easily found his house. It was set on a large piece of property surrounded by mature shrubbery, with a lawn that was neatly trimmed. She pulled into the driveway and cut the motor. Why wasn't there an outside light for her?

She hurried up the path. The house, too, was dark. Could it be Dennis wasn't home? She rang the bell. And heard chimes inside. She waited a decent interval. With no answer, she rang again.

Tapping her toe impatiently, she rang a third time.

At last a light switched on, and the door swung open. She stared at Dennis. He looked annoyed, irritated, as if she'd disturbed him at an inopportune time. He wore a hip-length blue velour robe that had parted to reveal a naked chest. From his skivvies down he was naked. His hair was damp, and he looked gorgeous. She had the sinking feeling she had interrupted him in the middle of a very private moment. Her gaze shot to his enigmatic gray eyes.

"You did say tonight?" she asked in a small voice.

Dennis stared back at her. He had waited for her, cursing himself for checking the time every few minutes. When he'd decided she wasn't coming, he'd turned off the downstairs lights and gone upstairs. When he'd heard the doorbell, he'd known she had come late to teach him another one of her lessons.

"No," he answered, "*you* said tonight. I'm accommodating you. Come in."

So much for pleasantries, Roxy thought as she followed him inside. Dennis had told her he was remodeling his old house in stages. To the left off the center hallway she saw a tastefully decorated living room, complete with a baby grand piano. On the marble ledge of a freestanding fireplace she spotted a pair of Steuben vases.

"Are you coming?" he asked.

She looked back at him. "Uh, yes." She wished he would close his robe. The mat of chest hair was boldly inviting. A lump of regret formed in her throat. She missed his smile, the tender teasing light that so often glinted in his eyes. "I didn't know you play the piano."

He shrugged. "There's a lot about me you don't know."

"You have a very nice home. Very restful."

There was an ironic twist to his lips. "Good, that's what I want my home to be."

He started up a winding staircase.

"Wait!" she cried, alarmed. "What about our appointment?"

He peered down at her. His expression was inscrutable, and she had a sudden ache to turn back the clock, to erase last night entirely.

"You're forty-five minutes late," he said, "so there is no appointment. If you want to talk, you're going to have to do it upstairs."

"Where?"

"My bedroom."

She tossed her head. "I'm not going up there."

"Suit yourself. You can leave or you can shout. I'm going back to my hot tub. When I'm home, I relax."

*Hot tub!*

Dennis continued up the stairs, his robe flapping at his sides. Remembering Shannon and Maggie, and alive with curiosity, she scrambled after him, getting a swift look at the modern paintings hanging on the walls.

He led her to a massive suite, and she wondered if her eyes were popping. Dennis's bedroom could best be described as a gracious living room that also contained a king-size platform bed. In addition to an entertainment center, it had a sofa, chairs, a wet bar, and a fireplace. She glanced up and saw the open ceiling above the bed. "Amazing!"

Dennis had been watching her closely, remembering how badly he had wanted to show her the house, especially his bedroom. He felt his whole body responding to her. She was so damned desirable, so beautiful. Rebelling against his desire, he tightened his jaw.

"The bathroom's through the dressing area," he said, "if you should need it."

Roxy couldn't resist peeking. In her list of

wishes she'd dreamed of a huge sunken tub with jets at various heights for a body massage. Dennis owned the most luxurious marble bathroom she'd ever seen in her life, and it was so large, she surmised it had originally been two rooms.

He touched her shoulder. Her head swung around, and their searching eyes met. Like two people who yearned to be more than strangers and were less than lovers, they felt the flare of desire, then forcibly banked it.

"Sorry," she murmured, drawing away from his magnetic touch.

He cleared his throat. "Just go through the louvered doors to the deck when you're done."

"No, it's okay. I'm coming with you."

He led her outside to a redwood deck. It was surrounded by a tall fence, secluding it from prying eyes. He tossed off his robe, and Roxy's mouth went dry. His tight derriere did more justice to his brief flesh-tone bathing suit than Michelangelo did to a statue. He lowered himself into the hot tub. In the shimmering water with lights reflecting off it, he was all molten gold and rippling muscles.

"I'm drinking soda," he said, glancing at her. "There's wine and strawberries in that small refrigerator. Help yourself."

A vase of American Beauty red roses sat atop the refrigerator, scenting the enclosure. Roxy was struck by the fact that Dennis surrounded himself with flowers. Wound up tighter than a coil, she poured herself a glass of wine.

"It's delicious," she said after taking a sip.

She remained standing, listening to a Billy Joel song coming over the outdoor speakers. She drank the wine faster than she normally would hoping to settle her nerves. The bubbling water was tempting, and she wished she were in it up to her neck. She finished her wine.

"What I came over to say . . ." she began as she poured herself another glass.

"Sit down," he said abruptly.

"Where?"

His arm shot out, indicating the white padded chair that held a stack of towels. "There."

Desperate to make peace—and hopeful he'd make a like effort—she asked if it would be all right to dangle her feet in the water.

Dennis knew she was trying to make it seem as if they were friendly. "Be my guest."

She removed her shoes and stockings. Bunching the hem of her skirt in one hand, she treated him to a quick glimpse of smooth thighs and long, shapely legs. Then she sat down, her feet and lower legs in the water. She swished her feet back and forth, wiggling her toes. It felt heavenly, and she said so.

Silence.

"What I tried to say earlier today," she went on, "is that I need a favor."

His face was closed. "I'm fresh out of favors."

She studied her hands. "It's not for me. I know how you feel about me. I wouldn't ask for myself."

There was a pause. "But you would for others?"

"Yes."

Their eyes met. Dennis kept his expression cool, distant, the exact opposite of the heat growing inside him. For an unguarded moment Roxy's eyes were yearning, then her gaze skittered away. She didn't speak. She just kept swishing her feet and released a heartfelt sigh.

"Oh, for goodness' sake!" he snapped. "Why don't you do what you're dying to do and get in the tub."

Roxy's heart thumped wildly. This was crazy. He was furious with her, yet he was inviting her to join him. She was eager, too, as he'd said. She just had to remember she was there for two serious reasons.

"I suppose that's all right," she said after a moment, "even though I don't have a swimsuit."

He shot her a look of pure disdain. "In Japan, Sweden, and other civilized countries, that wouldn't be a problem. It's only a problem if you make it one."

She shed her skirt, glad her blouse was long and covered her hips, then accepted his outstretched hand, and stepped daintily over the rim. She promptly got her blouse soaking wet.

"That was dumb," she muttered, looking woefully down at herself. "I didn't allow for the water's depth."

Dennis clenched his hands to keep from touching her satiny thigh. "Take it off. I'll put it in the dryer for you."

"I'm fine."

"Suit yourself."

As relaxing as the water was, Dennis's proximity sent all her nerves into high anxiety again. She hung on to her wineglass, taking big gulps, while Dennis leaned back and watched her. He was like a big silver cat, she mused, ready to pounce at his convenience.

The warmth of the wine spread through her insides, as the hot water heated her externally. Battling her nerves, she chanced a look at Dennis. His gaze was somber, disinterested. So much for looking sexy in his eyes, she thought. Apart from providing him with anger, he was clearly unmoved by her feminine charms. So why shouldn't she soak in the hot tub without her blouse? She stripped it off, leaving herself clothed only in a lacy bra and silky panties.

She glanced at him again. His eyes were hooded, now half-closed, as if to shut her out. She had disturbed his tranquillity, his sanctuary, and he obviously resented that.

"Do you do this every night?" she asked.

"As often as I can."

She nodded, as if he'd said something momentous. Continuing the meaningless chitchat, she replied, "I'd be in it daily if I owned it. It's fabulous. I'm sorry I made you cut short your date."

"You didn't."

She clamped her mouth shut and stared at the fence opposite her. Dennis took the opportunity to study her. Her skin glistened. Steam created a riot of curls in her red hair. Bathed by moonlight, her green eyes were luminous. He should feel better for letting her think he had been out with another woman. He didn't. He doubted if he would ever feel complete joy again. Roxy had never looked more tense, desirable, or beautiful, and he had never wanted her so much. He hadn't thought of another woman since he met her. He was horny as hell, and this ludicrous situation was not helping. They were sitting side by side in a hot tub, scantily clothed, their legs, arms, and shoulders all but touching. They were in the rear of the house, cloistered from curious eyes by a high fence and tall trees. It was the perfect setting for a romantic interlude, complete with wine, song, and starlight. The throbbing in his groin worsened. Looking at her full, inviting breasts didn't help. Wanting to put his mouth on them and taste their sweetness made it worse.

Roxy struggled to think of the best way to bring up her reason for being there. Her emotions careening and clashing, she settled for a simple request. "Can't we be friends?"

Dennis was painfully aware of her attempts to get an easy conversation started, so she could lead up to the favor that had brought her there.

"I have friends," he said.

She recoiled visibly, as if struck. Tears shimmered in her eyes, and the anger drained out of him. She was a guest in his house, and he was making it worse. "All right. Truce."

Roxy sighed with relief.

"I'm glad," she said simply. She wished he had said they could be friends but understood why he hadn't.

She gulped down the rest of her wine. "You never said you owned a hot tub." Glancing at him, she added. "I imagine your dates love it."

"I wouldn't know. It was only recently installed. You're the first."

A thrill ran through her at his words. Somewhere in the recesses of her mind she knew she had been handing herself excuses each time she phoned him. The moonlight supplied a silvery glow, and the wind crooned a soft sonata. The heated water swirled around them, until at last they succumbed to their bodies' demands. Somehow her head found a resting place in the crook of his arm. Smiling, she snuggled closer. His lips grazed her cheek. She liked hearing him say no other woman had been in the hot tub with him, even though technically speaking, she wasn't a date. He brushed a lock of her hair from her forehead.

Roxy glanced down at herself, at her puckered nipples, visible through her lace bra. She might as well be naked, yet it felt natural and right to be there with Dennis.

"We should talk," she said.

His lips touched her damp, soft cheek. "Wait until this song ends."

"Yes, of course." The night sky was vast, swept over by a wide brush of constellations. She listened as the Judds sang "Love Can Build a Bridge." Under other circumstances the lyrics could have been written for them. When the song ended, she asked, "May I have more wine, please?"

"I think you've had enough." He crossed his legs to hide his burgeoning erection. "You're tired and you're the designated driver."

She touched his hand, looking at him with unconscious coyness. "Would you drive me home?"

A smile teased his mouth as he thought of an alternative suggestion, then he brought himself under control. "No. If I did that, who would drive me home?"

"I hadn't thought of that." She paused. "Dennis?"

"Yes?"

"This is lovely."

He watched the supple motion of her breasts as she lifted her arm to brush back her hair. The air crackled with tension. Cravings pumped through him, and as she bumped up against him, she raised her face to his. Questioning, tentative, magically tense, the emotions he saw in her eyes mirrored what he felt. He wanted to ask her to stay, to give them another chance, but the words died unspoken. He would not humiliate himself by asking, even though he was drowning in desire.

Minutes ticked by. Moonlight streamed onto them, highlighting them, as if they were actors in a play who had momentarily forgotten their lines.

In truth, Roxy hadn't. She was simply too nervous, too afraid to speak them. In characteristic honesty she knew why she was in the water beside him, why she had removed her clothes, just as she knew the feeble excuses she had given herself not to make love with Dennis were empty. It wasn't merely his body that tempted her. His goodness attracted her. She had been waiting for him all her life.

She faced the truth, faced what had been building inside her. Today had been one of the worst days of her life. Racked with guilt, she had missed Dennis's laugh, his teasing. And she'd known he wouldn't come to her, not after the way she had trampled his pride. Filled with anxiety, she told herself to take the risk, to cross the chasm. If she didn't seize the moment, it would be gone. Forever. Still, facing the real possibility of rejection, she hesitated. Wasn't it better to deal with her private demons alone?

Seemingly impervious to the debate going on in her brain, her hand drifted down to rest lightly on his.

Dennis stiffened. His suspicious gaze swept her face. He reined in his instinct to ask her what trick she was up to now, as his hand, acting of its own volition, wrapped around hers.

Roxy trembled. Dennis hadn't yanked his hand away. He was helping her—willing her!—to find the courage to make things right between them.

She cleared her throat and looked up at him. "Dennis, I'm sorry for hurting you last night. I know you must think me a tease, but I'm not. You never did anything but be kind to me. If it's any consolation, I hurt myself as well."

He remained stoically silent, and Roxy wished he would say something, anything, to break the tension. He didn't. He was making her say it all. If not for his thumb slowly sweeping across her palm, she would have stopped.

Then the meaning of his action dawned on her. He was talking to her. Without saying a word, he was communicating to her, telling her that if she would just say what was in her heart and not be afraid, it would be all right. In a deep surrendering sigh she set aside her fears and lifted her free hand to caress his cheek.

"I don't want to go home," she said. "I can't stand us being cold strangers. I hated breakfast this morning, sitting there with Maggie and Louey and not being able to talk freely with you. I tried so hard not to let our bodies touch. I want to stay here. With you. For you. I need you to make love to me. If you still want to, that is. I'll understand if you refuse." Unable to go on, she dropped her hand.

The moon shone on her face. Looking at her tearstained eyes, her quivering lips, Dennis stopped resisting her. He cupped her chin in his hand.

"Even believing I was out on a date tonight?"

Her lips tightened, but she nodded. "Yes."

She ground it out with such obvious disgust, he laughed. Then he smothered her mouth in a kiss so devouring that when he ended it, they were both shaking.

"I had dinner with Steven Ostner tonight," he said. "I'm afraid I wasn't the best company."

"I thought you were with another woman."

"I know."

She wiped away her tears. Grinning, she said, "Whew! That was the hardest speech I've ever made in my whole life."

"And the most welcome." He kissed her again. "I couldn't stand this morning either."

"Dennis, do you remember the last things you said to me in the attic?"

He looked deeply into her eyes. In an emotion-tinged voice he said, "Every word. I told you I want to make love to you."

He rained a path of kisses from her eyes to her mouth. "I want to see your face next to mine when I awake."

He placed a soft, sultry kiss on her lips. "I want you to spend the night in my arms. All night. Will you spend the night?"

She read the lingering doubt in his eyes. She had come this far. There would be no turning back. They would have it all, together. Just as he promised. "Yes."

Dennis didn't hesitate. He helped her out of the water, then wrapped himself and her in a thick terry-cloth towel. He carried her into the bedroom, where he helped her shed the last of her clothes. He stripped off his suit and joined her on the bed, gathering her close.

He dipped his head, licking the last droplets of water from her neck and from the tender valley between her breasts. He kissed first one rosy crest, then the other.

He eased away to let his gaze sweep boldly over her. "You're beautiful."

"So are you," she replied. He was, she thought. More than magnificent. He was the most splendid man in the world. She sought no words of love, no promises for tomorrow. Tonight was theirs.

"Can you see the North Star if you retract the ceiling farther?" she asked.

He pressed the button, revealing more of the velvety night. He pointed to the North Star. "That and the heavens. We'll see them together."

Her eyes glowed like the stars. Then her eyelids fluttered closed as the magic began. . . .

Dennis led her to ecstasy with adoring hands and lips and loving words of praise. He supped on her body as if it were the finest wine. She gave herself up to him completely, knowing her mind and body were one with his.

Her breasts ached, yearning for his touch. He aroused her to a feverish pitch, taking a taut nipple into his mouth and tugging gently. His hand went to her secret place, parting her legs and gently invading. Then not so gently, but masterfully. She arched and writhed against him, her excitement heightening.

Caressing hands stroked her buttocks, then smoothed over the curve of her hips to pull her forward to his hard, demanding body. He wanted her so much it hurt, and wanted to make slow, languorous love to her. But as her restless hands and lips wantonly duplicated his stimulating seduction, his breathing became a tortured gasp. Gazing at his fiery angel, he lowered himself over her and parted her thighs. Her mouth was swollen from his kisses, her hair plundered by his fingers.

"Open your eyes, Roxy."

The second she did, he joined with her, burying himself in her hot, wet warmth. His hand touched her face as he stared lovingly into her eyes. Slowly, he began to stroke her. He thrust deeper and deeper, finding her core as her body arched upward. Their rhythm quickened. The only sounds in the room were sounds of passion. Gasps of breaths and murmurs, shared utterances of pleasures.

Driven by fate, by forces spinning them upward, they flew higher still. Above the bed the stars blazed across the heavens.

Magic dust drifted down, on them.

She clung to the sinewy muscles of his arms and rode to the heavens with him, where in perfect unison they cried out their ecstasy.

Blessed by a miracle of their making, they lingered with kisses and murmurs of thanks. Then, curled against her, he drew the blanket over her shoulders. His hand cupping her breast, they slept.

Content.

Hours later Roxy awoke with a start. Disoriented, she didn't know where she was at first. She knew only that she couldn't move and that she was more comfortable than she'd been in years. A leg and an arm held her down. She turned her head slightly, and her cheek met a stubbled chin.

She smiled, recalling Dennis carrying her to bed and, after making sure to protect her, making passionate love to her. She moved her hand along his bare flank.

"Dennis?"

He chuckled, his fingertips skimming her bare skin. "Who were you expecting?"

"Please. I remember drinking more wine in the middle of the night. I don't remember falling asleep."

He feigned shock. "You do remember making love a second time, don't you?"

She blushed. "Of course. It was wonderful. Thank you for relaxing me."

He kissed the soft spot behind her ear. His hands drifted over her tummy, then traced her slender form, worshiping it gently. "You're welcome. I'll give you a card with my hours and fee. Whenever you're tense, give me a buzz."

"I just may do that," she joked.

The bluish haze of dawn was creeping through the window. She cradled her head on his chest and idly plucked at a golden hair. "Dennis?"

"Mmmm?"

She rubbed her leg along his calf. "Do you remember what else you said in the attic?"

"Tell me," he said, hoping she remembered too.

She sprawled on top of him. Dennis was hard. And beautiful. The same desire that had flared before erupted anew.

"If I remember correctly," she murmured, "you said you wanted me to wake you up."

"For what reason?" He cupped her head, bringing it down to inhale her heady fragrance.

"I think I can find a good reason." Straddling him, she fit herself to him like a glove. With a little chuckle she began to rock sensuously.

Holding her hips down, he lifted his higher, catching her rhythm. "I was sure you could. . . ."

# *Eight*

The sun streamed through the sliding glass door, casting a brilliant shaft of light into the room. Roxy shifted to her side, her hair tangled in Dennis's fingers as he listened to Shannon's plight.

"Isn't this out of the ordinary for you?" he asked. "From what you tell me, she wasn't a battered wife."

"She has four children, one of whom is an infant. Between her husband's death, the fire that destroyed her home and business, and the insurance company that's dragging its feet with her claim, she qualifies. Life is battering her. Can you help them? The poor mother is beyond fatigue. John, the oldest, tries to be the man of the house, but she needs your special talents, not a child's."

Dennis chuckled. "Do you approve of my special talents?"

Roxy wiggled. His special talents had kept her weak and willing all night and morning. He had made her feel like a goddess instead of an ordinary woman. "What do you think?"

His hand strayed to her firm breast, then downward to a softly rounded hip. "I think this can get to be a pleasurable habit." He sighed. "Okay. Back to business. I have a few friends who are insurance adjusters. She can hire one to represent her in her loss. Naturally, her insurance company has its own adjusters. Hers will keep theirs honest. She'll need an independent contractor to estimate the cost of replacing her house, interiors included. She'll have to work from memory on certain things, but it can be done. As to the waiver of premiums on her husband's life insurance, if she gets an affidavit from the doctor who signed the original letter stating his medical injury, I'll take it from there. As far as her business losses are concerned, she knows who her suppliers are. We'll get copies of her bills from them to determine loss. It's a paper trail, but it's not insurmountable."

Roxy smiled. "You make it sound so easy. I knew you were the right man."

"I accept my share of thanks," he said immodestly.

"Oh," she teased, responding to the subtle pressure of his hand on her spine. Whisper-light, she kissed his shoulder, then leaned back to admire the long, sinewy line of his hard thigh.

"Exactly how do you expect *Shannon* to repay you?"

For a long moment Dennis mused over his reply, all the while applying talented hands to sweep across her soft flesh. His lips found a sensitive crevice at the base of her neck, then trailed upward to tease her ear.

She groaned. "We have to talk."

His hand curved around her nape. "Later."

"No. Please, Dennis, now. I'm leaving soon."

He balked and sat up. "You're not going any-place. Maybe you're satisfied, but I'm not. You used the answering machine last night, and the world didn't end. You said Nina knew you were coming here. Well, if there were an emergency, she'd call you here. She hasn't, so you aren't needed."

"That's true," she allowed.

"Good, then call your mom and tell her you've had a change of plans. I'm declaring a weekend holiday for the two of us."

She wouldn't think of refusing him. "All right, but I still need to check in. Besides, I need a change of clothes."

"Fair enough. While you do that, I'll speak with Shannon, prepare her for what she'll need to do. We can call the insurance adjuster from your place. He works at home on Saturdays. Inci-dentally"—he paused to leer at her—"my fantasies include taking a bath and having you scrub my back."

He placed a solid kiss on her mouth. "What? No thanks from the water nymph? Treat me right," he teased, wiggling his eyebrows, "and I'll let you turn on all the jets."

Roxy wouldn't allow herself to be dissuaded by humor. She forcefully tamped down the urge to explore his body again. What she had to say about Maggie meant more now than it would have before last night, before she and Dennis had made love. They had shared the most intimate act two people could engage in, experiencing it together in per-fect harmony, yet, she couldn't begin to guess what his reaction would be when she spoke about Maggie. She clutched the edge of the blanket.

Dennis frowned at her. "Roxy, stop twisting the blanket. What's troubling you?"

"I'm concerned about Maggie."

"Why? She's got a job. She and Louey will do fine."

Roxy jumped at the opening Dennis gave her, mustering her most professional tone. "You're right. She's made a beginning. A small step in the right direction. For her and for Louey."

"That's what I said. So what's the problem?"

She took a deep breath. "I think it's unwise for you to date her."

Dennis's brows rose so high, they met his hairline. Considering where they were, her statement took him aback. Cautiously optimistic, he suspected the reason behind her request.

"Why?" He kept his tone bland.

*Why?* Lowering her eyes, Roxy didn't see the glint of humor in his. She should have known he would resent her intrusion into his private affairs. She felt a momentary agony and almost retreated, but the pain of thinking of Dennis with Maggie was too much for her to bear. Dennis hadn't spoken of love to her. Not that she would have believed him if he had. Infatuations happened with lightning speed. Love didn't. Infatuations usually carried time limits, following a comet's path of fire and flash.

Dennis was a marvelous, exciting lover. A woman could easily believe that the lavish attention he paid to her was love. Being mature, discreet, and circumspect, Roxy didn't. She guessed his hungry need of her was a combination of lust and infatuation. As magical as the night had been, she wouldn't let it turn her head.

"I just don't think," she answered him, "that Maggie's ready for a man like you."

Dennis propped himself up on an elbow, winding a lock of Roxy's hair around his finger. She tried to get up, but he held her back with a firm arm. When she lay down again, he drew a lazy pattern on her skin.

"A man like me?" he repeated.

"Yes," she muttered. "Now let's drop the subject."

"No, we won't. You started this, not I. Not only do I practice safe sex, I try my best to satisfy a woman." He could hardly keep a straight face. "Were you satisfied? You weren't faking it, were you?"

"No," she mumbled. "I mean yes, I was satisfied, and no, I wasn't faking it."

"A lot satisfied or a little?"

She felt absurd and sincerely wished she hadn't brought up the subject. "Couldn't you tell? A whole lot. You're very sexy. Very considerate."

He breathed an audible sigh of relief. "You can't know how good that makes me feel, especially since I can return the compliment. You're quite a hot number. Did you know that when you have an orgasm, you tighten your muscles in a way that drives me crazy?"

She couldn't answer as her face turned beet red.

"Getting back to your request," he went on, "if you can give me a sensible reason not to date Maggie, I'll consider doing what you ask."

Mortified and completely misunderstanding his meaning, she scowled at him. Obviously, he wasn't about to let her off the hook.

"That shouldn't be hard for an outspoken woman like you," he prompted. "Go ahead, sweet. Say whatever is on your pretty little mind."

She glowered. "I'll scratch your eyes out if you touch her. There! Is that outspoken enough for you?"

He smothered a laugh. "You care that much for Maggie?"

"No. Yes. No. I mean yes. Oh, hell!"

"Which is it?" He leaned over to kiss her pouty lower lip, dragging his tongue back and forth across it. Knowing how sensitive her breasts were, he whisked his thumb over her nipple, then lowered his head to kiss it.

From there, he landed a love bite on her tummy. "Don't keep me in suspense. Which is it?"

"Stop that." She groaned. "I'm serious."

"I'm sure you are. Don't blame me for being curious. I want to know why after spending the night having glorious sex with me, and now lying naked in my arms, you would mention Maggie?"

Roxy yanked up the blanket, steeling herself for what she had to say. "Maggie's vulnerable. Before she can think of being with a man—intimately, that is—she should get her life back together."

Dennis pulled down the blanket, and his hand drifted along her thigh. "Before," he repeated casually, and Roxy cringed. "You figured that out all by yourself, did you?"

"Someone has to protect these women." She was miserable.

"Fine. I'll wait a few months. Then Maggie won't be defenseless, susceptible, or as you put it, vulnerable to my charms. Her life will be on track. She'll be ready for me. Does that please you?"

He watched her covertly. Her cheeks were flaming, her eyes flashing. Yes, he thought, Roxy was definitely jealous. "Well?" he asked. "Does that please you, Roxy?"

She exploded. "No, dammit! It does not please me!"

Unable to stem his delight, he drew out the sweet victory. "What would please you?"

Too angry to speak, she pressed her lips together.

He grinned. "I can't hear you. However, if it makes you happier, I'll leave Maggie alone. I'll confine my attention to women who, as you put it, are ready for me. In fact, if you give me a list of women to date, I'll be happy to take them out. That should please you."

Fire ignited in Roxy's eyes. "Well, it doesn't."

"Temper, temper," he chided. "It's true what they say about redheads. You, my pet, possess a nasty temper. The only time I can count on your being nice is when you're sleeping or we're making love."

"Let me up."

"No way." His gentle banter ceased. He took his finger to lift her chin, forcing her to look at him. "If I have to hog-tie you to this bed, you're going to admit the truth. Stop lying to yourself and to me."

She tried to buck him off her, but he didn't budge.

"Admit it," he said.

She glared at him. "All right. If you want the truth, I don't want you making any woman feel the way you make me feel when you're inside me."

Dennis grinned. He relaxed his hold on her, kissing her eyes, her cheeks, her mouth. She couldn't have paid him a more welcome compliment. Roxy, his feisty, fiery angel, might not admit it, but she was jealous as hell.

He turned to the vase of roses he'd carried in from the deck and set on the nightstand beside the bed. Pulling one blossom off its stem, he scattered the petals on her breasts. "Thank you," he said gently. "I won't date other women. You're more than enough for me. Besides, you're too late.

I already phoned Nina and told her I wouldn't be going to her party."

Roxy's eyes widened. "You did?"

He kissed the tip of her nose. "I did."

"Why did you let me say all that for nothing?" she wailed.

"It wasn't for nothing. Darling, what makes you think I'd want anyone else? The Fates would be furious with me. Now, of course, we can go together."

His conversation with Nina the day before had also included her thoughts about the shelter. She had repeated Roxy's dream to provide care for as many battered women as possible. More numbers meant more hours of commitment. She mentioned the impracticality of working understaffed on a shoestring budget, and of finding funds in a tight economy. She concluded by saying they needed either to win the lottery or find a fairy godmother who could wave a wand and produce larger quarters.

"I hope that closes the subject of other women," he said to Roxy.

His hands began to move over her, restarting the magic. She saw the luminous light of longing in his eyes. His lips skimmed across hers.

"What am I going to do?" she whispered. Caution had been her second nature for so long, she didn't know how to handle her tumultuous reaction to Dennis, or her body's wanton usurping of her self-control. "One minute you make me furious, the next you make my heart beat like a drum."

Dennis didn't share Roxy's confusion. What she conveniently called infatuation, he truthfully called love. He was in it. Deeply. From the tips of his toes to the top of his head. Roxy captivated him. She filled his dreams. When he'd thought he'd lost her, he'd been nearly catatonic with misery. She was the epicenter of his life, but he wasn't ready to tell her that. Not until she knew herself better. She would be astounded if she knew how quickly he'd fallen in love with her. For now he was simply grateful she trusted him with her body. Gaining her heart's trust would be another battle.

"I suppose," he murmured, continuing to explore her supple body with his lips, "there's only one way to cure your problem."

To her infinite pleasure, he did.

She was asleep when he went downstairs to bring in the newspaper. After he made a few phone calls, arranging for a spectacular, memorable night for Roxy and him, he sat down at the kitchen table with a cup of coffee and the real estate section. He circled several possible apartments for Maggie. When he finished, he took advantage of the solitude to think about the compassionate redhead sleeping in his bed. In many ways she was a contradiction, and that raised questions in his mind.

For example, why would she submerge her own healthy desires and completely dedicate herself to serving others? Alice's death held the key. He sensed this whenever Roxy mentioned her sister's name. Which made him wonder about Alice. Why wasn't Roxy active in an organization that spotlighted the dangers of driving while under the influence of alcohol? Why abused women? And why such total commitment? He had nothing against allegiance to a cause, provided it left time for privacy.

So where did that leave him? What did he want?

His entire body could answer that question. Before Roxy, he had always taken his pleasure with women merely to satisfy his body and theirs. His heart wasn't involved. Last night had taught him he could never return to his former ways. Roxy was his future. She awakened every fiber of his being to a new awareness, and that was due to love.

Roxy was color and passion. He remembered the overwhelming wonder in her deep emerald eyes after they made love. So what did he want most of all? He wanted her to move in with him so they could build on their beginning, continue to love each other, but equally important, talk. About everything. Their lives. The day's events. Their hopes. Their fears.

He didn't relish being apart from her, even for a few days. He wanted her with him when he testified at the trial in California. Roxy could use a change, anyway. And they needed time together, quality time in an atmosphere conducive to intimacy and sharing. Although he enjoyed doing things on the spur of the moment, by nature he was a planner. Which made his meeting Roxy all the more unusual. A slow smile tugged his lips. He should pay homage to her parachute, though he'd prefer to do so while packing it away forever. She had so quickly become an essential part of his life. Happiness welled up in him. He shook his head in amazement and went back to his task of finding Maggie an apartment.

Awash in a sea of sensual reminisces, Roxy snuggled beneath the covers. She felt so peaceful, she hated to get up. She burrowed beneath the blanket and pressed the button to retract the ceiling. Last night Dennis had taken her to the stars and beyond. She tingled pleasurably and watched a fluffy white cloud move across her vision. Behind it the sun shone in a powder-blue sky. Her gaze went to the clock on the dresser. She was shocked at how late she'd slept. Regretfully, she got out of bed and showered. When she couldn't find her clothes, she borrowed Dennis's velour bathrobe. The material carried his inviting masculine scent.

Rolling up the sleeves and with her stomach rumbling from hunger, she went downstairs in search of her host. The aroma of coffee guided her to the kitchen. He owned a culinary artist's array of pots and pans, which hung from hooks above the island counter. The modern decor in the pristine room looked straight out of *House and Garden*. Not like her clean but cluttered kitchen, with its stacked countertops.

Unaware he was being observed, Dennis leaned into the open refrigerator, one arm flung over the top of the door. In profile, his features were strongly etched. His golden hair, as undisciplined as ever, flopped over his forehead. He wore skivvies, a T-shirt, and slippers. She watched the play of muscles in his powerful frame and grinned appreciatively.

"Nice buns."

He swiveled, smiling broadly. "If my memory serves, and I assure you it does, your tempting tush is as glorious as the rest of you. Did you sleep well?"

"Fabulously."

"You're welcome." He took her in his arms and kissed her, then licked his lips, relishing the aftertaste. "Mmmm, sinfully delicious." He nuzzled her neck. "You smell nice. What are you wearing?"

"Basic me. Milkweed. Oil of wintergreen and cloves, dabbed in strategic places."

"All that." He grinned. "We should bottle it for perfume. It's bound to be a hit."

She sighed deeply. "You shouldn't have let me sleep."

The corners of his eyes crinkled with his smugly satisfied smile. "You needed it."

Color flooded her cheeks. His enthusiastic love-making, and her eager participation in it, had knocked her out. "I need my clothes."

"You don't hear me complaining. Roxy, sit down. Let's be regular people. I'd like it if we talked."

"About what?"

He took a chance. "About your sister. About what you haven't told me."

Avoiding his gaze, she sat at the table. "I'm a zombie without my coffee."

He poured her a mugful. "Roxy, all I know about her is the cause of her death. Was she the reason you gave up teaching?"

Her fingers tightened on the mug. "How did you know I taught school? Did Nina tell you?"

With some reluctance he told her about seeking his friend's father's help.

Sheepishly, she admitted she had asked Bob to check up on him for her. Although he was startled, Dennis said she'd done the right thing.

She nodded. "I had to. You see . . . my brother-in-law abused my sister. Alice couldn't break through her barrier of shame, and she hid the truth. She didn't know it was okay to reach out for help. I only learned after she died, when I found a letter to me that she'd never mailed, how horrible it had been for her. Do you know how awful it made me feel to know I hadn't been there for her?"

She started weeping, and Dennis gathered her in his arms, stroking her back until she was ready to continue. In a choked-up voice she told him that her sister had been pregnant when she died, and that her parents were unaware that Tom had abused her. "They were grieving for their first-born, for the grandchild they would never see. What would be the point of telling them? Giving my home over to Safe Havens happened gradually. I never intended to stop teaching."

"Why did you, darling?"

A few more tears spilled from her eyes. Being in Dennis's embrace was like being anchored in a safe port. Her cheek rested on his chest, and she could hear the steady, strong beating of his heart.

"It happened by circumstance, not design, starting with one of my students. He was a sweet little boy whose personality underwent a drastic change. He was turning into a bully, shoving and kicking, destroying other children's property. I set up a parent conference. His mother broke down when I asked her if there were problems at home. She said that if she didn't get her son away from his father, he would turn out like him. I'd never actually talked to a victim of abuse before. When she rolled up her sleeves, her arms were black and blue. Her thighs were too. That's how the bastard she married got his jollies. No woman should take such abuse. We spoke about DYFUS, the Division of Youth and Family Services. The school social worker coordinated the case. Predictably, her husband blamed me. He even filed charges that I'd wrecked his happy home. Thankfully, the case never came to court."

"What happened to the woman?"

"She received counseling, was given shelter, and ultimately divorced her husband. The judge granted her full custody and issued a restraining order against her ex-husband. She was lucky. She received help. Two months later Alice died. I wasn't there for her."

Roxy began to shake again. Dennis soothingly stroked her back and kissed her forehead. She snuggled into his arms as if she belonged there. "I'm so sorry," he murmured.

"Alice's fear to speak out caused me to research the reasons why many women keep silent, why they stay in abusive marriages. They feel lost, alone. For many it would be financially disastrous to leave. I had to do something to help break the cycle."

"I think you're wonderful," Dennis said, meaning it sincerely.

She was calm now, the agitation gone from her eyes. "You're pretty terrific too. Thanks for listening. Sharing this has lifted a weight from my shoulders."

She kissed him, then slipped off his lap to phone Nina and her mother.

"That was easy," she said after she'd hung up. "Both of them told me to have fun." She grinned. "So I will."

They prepared breakfast side by side, telling each other preposterous tales they dredged up from their childhoods. Roxy told him she went through a tomboy stage, then a cowboy stage, when she preferred a lasso to a doll.

"Thank goodness for me you got over that!" Dennis declared, and kissed her to remind her of her femininity. He was appalled when she told him she took her first parachute jump at age eight. She flew off a second-story porch, landing on a clump of hedges that broke her fall.

"It hooked me," she said, grinning.

He didn't think it was funny. "If you were my kid, I'd have tanned your hide."

She giggled. "My parents beat you to it."

Both bragged shamelessly, lying with straight faces. Dennis declared himself a champion bowler. "Three hundred is my norm."

Roxy pronounced her wizardry at poker. "I'm good for at least four royal flushes in five hands."

On the subject of food Dennis told the truth. He favored Italian. She said she loved Chinese food. He admitted he had never developed a taste for it.

Are you a good cook?" she asked as she cracked eggs into a frying pan, careful to keep the yolks intact.

"The best," he said.

"So am I," she said, equally immodest. "Stew isn't my only specialty."

He nuked the bacon to death and mistakenly doubled the amount of water for the can of orange-juice concentrate. She burned the toast and flipped his eggs over too hard, ruining both centers.

It was the best breakfast either ever ate.

When she was done, she carried her dishes to the sink. "What happens if you go above the third floor?"

Dennis paused in putting the butter back in the refrigerator. "Huh?"

"The third floor of a hotel?" she prodded at his blank expression. When he still stared uncomprehendingly, she exploded with laughter. "You faker. You told me you get nosebleeds above the third floor."

"I do."

"You do not. What happens when you fly?"

Pretending to be stung, he reacted with a hurt look. "From a hero to a scoundrel in two seconds. Roxy, my sweet, you're fickle."

She stuck out her tongue. "You're a sucker for sympathy."

"Is it working?"

She giggled. "I'm afraid so."

That deserved a long kiss. When they drew apart, both were breathing hard.

"I guess we're going to have to do it," he said with mock sadness.

She looked down at his rigid arousal and felt an answering need melting her core. "I suppose it's the least I can do to relieve your suffering."

"I appreciate the sacrifice. Think of it as your morning exercise, working off your meal."

Grabbing her hand, he blazed a path upstairs. Clothes were abandoned, replaced by feverish kisses, seeking hands, hungry lips. They came together lustfully, wildly, explosively. His suckling mouth found her sensitive breasts.

"Do you like this?" he whispered, reveling in her moans of delight.

"Oh, yes," she purred. "Don't stop."

Moments later, she returned his generosity. "That feels good," he told her. "Roxy, you're driving me crazy."

She squeezed him gently. "Shall I stop?"

"I'll die if you do."

She didn't.

He rolled on top, nudging apart her thighs.

"Kiss me, Dennis. Touch me."

"My pleasure."

An ecstasy later, she arched higher, receiving him. He felt her incredible heat with each strong, rhythmic thrust. She cried out, digging her hands into his back. "Dennis . . ."

He loved to watch her eyes glaze with rapture. She was hot and his. "I know, love. I feel it too."

Each was determined to give to the other. In so doing, both received more than they ever dreamed possible.

# *Nine*

Minutes passed in silence.

Roxy lay facedown on the sheets. She knew her cheeks were as red as her hair. As red as the rest of her body must be. If she had wanted to convince Dennis that one touch, one look from him, would have her racing upstairs and wantonly offering herself to him, she couldn't have done a better job.

Lifting her hair to the side, he nibbled her neck. Then he leaned against the pillows, his hand resting possessively on her shoulder.

"It's okay to look at me, Roxy. You weren't alone just then. We both shared that shattering climax."

When she didn't answer, he gazed at her thoughtfully. Last night she had given herself permission to make love with him. This morning he had initiated it. She had let her emotions rule her, and she didn't like it.

He patted her shoulder. "Roxy, don't do this to yourself. To us."

She turned over, staring at him with large green eyes. "Dennis, I don't make a habit of acting like a sex bunny."

He grinned. "I don't either. If we're smart, we'll keep our secret between the two of us, then we won't have to share."

His humor helped dissolve her tension. "Can I interest you in a communal bath?"

At his nod, she dashed into the bathroom to turn on the water in the tub. "Where are we going today?" she called back to him.

"We're going to find Maggie an apartment," he said, sauntering into the bathroom naked.

"How will she cover the first month's rent and the deposit?"

"We'll work it out."

"Meaning, you'll advance the money." She stepped into the tub and sighed with pleasure. "You're a nice man."

"After we find an apartment, we'll come back here and make love until we're too weak to move."

It sounded wonderful.

"Luxury," she murmured later, as they passed the fifteen-minute mark of luxuriating in a scented bubble bath, "is soaking until your skin looks like prunes."

He sent a slew of bubbles in her direction. Her skin would never remotely resemble a prune's. It glistened and glowed, and soapsuds clung to her breasts. "I think I'm in heaven," he said. "I'm totally at peace."

At least he was until he remembered, a few seconds later, to tell her that Steven Ostner would definitely feature Safe Havens in a Sunday supplement.

"That's wonderful!" she cried. "Now I've got to figure out a way to make it special. Otherwise, the article will read like one more hard-luck story."

Having said that, she grew increasingly reflective. Dennis could almost see the wheels spinning in her head.

"What is that brain of yours cooking?" he asked.

She snapped out of her daze. "I was thinking . . ."

She outlined her idea, growing increasingly enthusiastic. The more zealous she became, the less Dennis liked it.

A minute later he shot up so fast, water sloshed onto the tile floor. "A rally?"

"Now look what you've done," she scolded. "A bath is supposed to relax you. Calm down and listen. A rally will give us a boost, a shot in the arm. I'll get a band."

"Who's going to foot the bill for this band?"

She leaned over the tub, patting the wet floor with the sponge. "Don't squeeze that thing back in the tub!" Dennis warned, seeing that she wasn't paying the least attention to what she was doing.

"Oops, sorry. The music teacher from the school I taught at is my friend. I'll ask him if he'll donate his time in exchange for free publicity."

"Where will this rally take place?"

She paused a scant second. "Outside city hall."

"What happens if it rains?"

"Bite your tongue. We'll have a rain date." She shook her head. "No, that won't work. The logistics would kill us." For a minute Dennis hoped she would abandon the idea, but then she brightened. "No problem. If it rains, the press will feel sorry for us. Don't forget they'll share in our drenching experience."

Dennis cursed, and she shook her finger at him.

"Dennis, the important thing is for the mayor and our elected officials to not only commit to helping abused women and children, but to have them outline the steps they're willing to take to lessen their plight. We'll ask the media to send reporters. Safe Havens needs all the good publicity it can get. We'll organize our ex-tenants. They'll want to help, I'm sure."

"Roxy, stop referring to them as tenants. Tenants pay rent. Most of your money flows in one direction. Out."

She was undaunted. "This should reverse the process. You can lead the rally with me."

"Whaaat?"

She squeezed his hand. "Darling, you weren't listening."

"Sweetheart." He clenched his teeth. "I did listen. I heard enough."

"Aren't you interested?"

"For you, yes. For me, no."

"Why? You're sympathetic. Look what you're doing for Maggie and Louey and Shannon and her kids. You've a very generous man."

"Behind the scenes, Roxy, not center stage. I'm a private person. I'll write you a check."

"Phooey. It's not like I'm asking you to skydive."

"Roxy." He glowered at her. "Don't mention skydiving and me in the same breath. That isn't the way into my good graces."

Her foot sensually rubbed his calf. "All I ask is for you to help me give my ladies the best fifteen minutes of fame possible. Your presence will show everyone you agree with our goals. If you refuse, I'll have to think of something else."

He gave her a skeptical look. "Not for me."

Before she could protest, he rose, signaling an end to the bath. Roxy let out her breath. Water sluiced off his body, delineating each hard muscle and making her mouth water. She followed him out, whipping a towel around her body and patting herself dry.

Dennis slung his towel around his hips. She chattered about her rally idea as he shaved. Finished, he strode back to the bedroom. She followed, still talking as he dressed in a yellow cotton shirt and khakis.

"Say something," she demanded at last. "Don't you think you're carrying this Mr. Conservative thing too far?"

"No."

"Haven't you ever attended a political rally?"

"What for? I read about the issues, party platforms, and past records. I listen to debates on television. Political rallies are a bunch of hype. I have better things to do with my time."

"Like what? What do you do?" She fastened her skirt and smoothed it down.

He kissed the tip of her nose. "I make love. That's why you're sleeping here tonight."

She sat down to slip on her shoes. "I can't do that. I have a business to run."

"Fine. I'll come to you. We'll make love in your bed in the attic. We can entertain your 'tenants' by crashing through the floor." He gave her a no-nonsense look. "I'm not kidding. I happen to like cuddling."

She arched her brows. "You happen to like what comes before the cuddling."

"Don't you?"

She did. And that was fine, as long as she recognized that what she felt was merely infatuation. "Okay, we'll compromise. Since you're helping me, I'll sleep here tonight."

He smiled slightly, aware that she needed a reason to convince herself to stay another night. "Promise?" She nodded. "Say it. You promise to sleep here tonight. And I'm holding my options open."

She shook her head. "Options! That's black-mail."

"Not if you want my help."

"All right. I promise."

"That's better."

"I said yes because of your hot tub and bath-room."

"You said yes because of my body."

She tossed her head. "That too."

He winked. "See what you can get when you compromise?"

"I compromised because I don't feel like spend-ing the night in a sleeping bag in my office."

Dennis decided to let her have the last word. He made the necessary phone calls to check that each apartment he'd circled would be available for viewing. Soon after they left his house, he learned that finding an appropriate apartment with Roxy was an adventure. He drove by several places he'd marked in the newspaper without bothering to stop, because she nixed each of them in short order.

"What's wrong with that one?" he asked after she'd crossed off the third condominium complex.

"No charm. Would you want to live there? The first one was a barracks. The second was a rabbit warren. That last one didn't keep up the grounds."

He had to agree with her. "When, and if, we ever stop," he said, "why don't you pretend to be my wife."

"Why?"

"I like it better than mistress."

She gave him a challenging look. "I'm not so sure myself. No, we'll tell the truth. We're apartment-hunting for a friend. A single mother with a child. We have to know if there are children for Louey to play with." She went on with her list of particulars. "We'll also have to check closets, countertops, cabinets, and cross-ventilation. Good plumbing and heating. Public transportation to get to your office. A school with a good reputation. Within walking distance of a super-market." She was iffy on the need for space to eat in the kitchen. "But a washer and a dryer would be great."

They ended up finding a two-bedroom apart-ment in a private home, with all the amenities plus its own side entrance. The owner was a widow with three grandchildren. Roxy fell in love with the yard.

"It's perfect for Louey," she said, then poked him. "There's even a jungle gym."

Dennis remembered he had promised to set up the one at Roxy's. "I promise to do it by next weekend."

They'd got most of what was on Roxy's list. The owner, a Mrs. Wilkins, understood Maggie would need to see it first. If everything was all right, she could move in immediately. Saying they would be back in a few hours, Dennis and Roxy drove to Safe Havens to tell Maggie and Louey.

For the second time in as many days, Maggie was overwhelmed. Dennis looked to Roxy for help. "She cries at the drop of a hat."

"I told you. It's because you're a nice guy."

"If that's so, you better kiss me. You did the last time you complimented me."

He quickly took control of the kiss that left her knees weak with his greedy passion.

"Later," he murmured. "Bring a dress for a fancy date. We're going out in style tonight. But I warn you. You have to be dressed and ready to go by five o'clock."

Roxy was surprised by the early hour, but too excited to bother asking why.

And she had the perfect outfit. A never-worn satin-trimmed silk chiffon strapless dress with a jacket of point d'esprit and reembroidered lace. One of her former guests was a talented seamstress. She had made it for Roxy as a present after she'd gotten her life back on track. It was a copy of a six-thousand dollar Bill Blass.

They collected Maggie and Louey and drove back to Mrs. Wilkins's house. Maggie and Louey loved the spacious apartment. The house was located on a quiet street with huge oak trees lining the sidewalks, yet within walking distance of a supermarket. Maggie could catch a bus only a few blocks away, and the school bus stopped right at the corner. While Maggie oohed and aahed over the clean rooms, the freshly laundered Priscilla curtains, the gleaming maple furniture, Roxy took Mrs. Wilkins aside and handed her a bag. Inside was a new box of crayons and a new coloring book.

"If you give Louey this," Roxy said, "he'll be your friend for life."

By the time they left, Louey had given Mrs. Wilkins a big hug, and she'd given him permission to call her Grandma.

When they returned to Roxy's house, Louey even invited Shannon's kids to visit him. Roxy left with a good feeling.

As Dennis drove away from Safe Havens, she said, "I wish I could solve all my problems as easily as you solved Maggie's."

Dennis was thinking the same thing about Roxy.

# *Ten*

Roxy and Dennis each wanted to surprise the other. He wouldn't tell her where they were going, and she refused to let him see her until she was completely dressed. The air of mystery and excitement spiked their pleasure. Before leaving his bedroom with his clothes, he gathered her to him, pulling the whole soft length of her to his hard body, fitting her hips to his. He gazed down at her perfectly shaped lips, which were curved in an impish smile, and gauged the excitement in her expressive eyes. Her hands rested on his hips. It was all he could do not to scoop her up in his arms and take her back to bed.

"Maybe we should stay home," he murmured.

Her hands glided up his back. "Do you want to?"

He laughed at her. She was dying to go out, and only asked to be polite.

He made a great show of giving in. "Later. You'll know exactly what's on my mind when we dance. I shall mentally strip you of your glamour togs, whisper naughty things in your ear, and generally make a pest of myself."

"I shall look like a hag," she teased, and shooed him out the door. Although she could no longer see him, he was there, his presence stamped everywhere in his room—and within her. A new dimension of feelings was taking root in Roxy's psyche, strong emotional ties that stunned, confused, and frightened her with their intensity. Never before had a man showered her with such adoration. She could still feel the tingling awareness from his parting caress, the press of his lips upon hers. Even his male fragrance swirled in her sensory self to fill her vial of memories. This date, this night, would be a keepsake. She sensed it and prepared for it like a bride.

In one short day they were living like a couple. They knew each other's bodies intimately. Often one would start a sentence and the other would know instinctively the root that prompted the thought. The depth of her infatuation scared her, and she reminded herself of its seductive but temporary status. Enjoy the now, she warned. Don't look at tomorrow.

With Dennis gone from the room, she unzipped the garment bag that held her dress. Her lace bra, panties, and stockings already on, she slipped the black dress over her head, then pulled on the long-sleeved jacket. Demure yet sexy, it was like a veiled caress of lace, and drew the eye down to the dress's strapless bodice. Her only jewelry was a pair of large glass earrings. She looked and felt glamorous. Tonight she wanted moonlight and stardust. She wanted to forget her attic room and the sleeping bag in her office, the endless government application forms, the harried late-night phone calls, the constant pleas for money, the sad faces of the women she saw daily. Tonight was hers to hoard in her memory book.

Dennis made it happen.

Dennis was Safe Havens's Pied Piper. Maggie sang his praises. Shannon and her children gazed at him with hope for the future in their eyes. He had been extraordinarily patient with Shannon and had brought along a tape recorder, leaving it with her to add information. Roxy marveled at his way with people. He was a born communicator, getting Shannon to open up and helping to prod her memory without putting pressure on her. His manner with John had showed both concern and respect for the youth.

She picked up her brush and tried different styles with her hair. She discarded the French chignon for a swept-back Spanish look, discarding that to wear it loose as Dennis preferred.

She slipped on her satin shoes. Tonight and tomorrow, she told herself, then back to reality. Feeling like a princess, she went in search of her prince.

She found him in the living room, his arm resting on the marble mantel above the fireplace. He was dressed in tuxedo finery, gold links at his cuffs, a snowy white shirt beneath his jacket. He turned and caught his breath. In her calculations to savor this night, she would always remember the intimate glow in his eyes when he saw her. They had both transformed themselves with costly apparel, displaying their splendor, yet underneath they were the same two people who increasingly couldn't bear to be apart.

Dennis came to her with both hands extended and pulled her gently to him so as not to muss her hair or mar her makeup.

"You're the loveliest woman I've ever seen." His husky voice betrayed his emotions.

She was sleekly beautiful, a flaming-haired

temptress with jeweled eyes. Her fragrance captivated him. He adored the pearly creaminess of her
skin. She was a defender, a Joan of Arc, and yet
sometimes she was a scared, uncertain woman.
She was a lady and a hoyden. She was everything
he wanted. A prize named Roxy Harris.

Because the warm glow in his eyes moved her so,
Roxy covered her nervousness by playfully preen-
ing. She batted her long lashes and slid her tongue
suggestively across her lower lip. Tonight she had
only one need, one desire—to be with Dennis. To
revel in her infatuation before she had to return the
glass slipper.

She smiled into eyes, loving their silvery color.
What she saw in them reflected his personality.
Strong and sure. Constant and valuable. Honest,
caring qualities Dennis carried with ease and
confidence.

He escorted her to the door, and she gasped
when she saw the white limousine at the curb. A
uniformed driver held open the rear door. Dennis
smiled with satisfaction at her surprise.

"Where are we going?" she asked as he slid in
beside her.

He handed her a single rose. "Ssshhh. Don't
spoil my surprise."

"Okay." She tried to remain calm, but the tapping of her toes and the way she peered out the
window gave her excitement away.

They were driven into Manhattan to the Plaza
Hotel where Dennis had booked a suite. As if by
magic, a suitcase with a nightgown, a change of
clothes, and shoes was produced by the driver. It
had been in the trunk.

"But when?" Roxy asked. "You weren't in my
room."

"Nina selected the clothes while we were at Mrs.
Wilkins's."

They were shown to a two-room suite with a blue striped sofa and chairs in the sitting room, and a fireplace, and crystal chandeliers in both the sitting room and bedroom. A dinner table gleamed with Baccarat crystal and Royal Copenhagen dinnerware. Dennis lit the candles while Roxy watched, stunned.

"I thought we were going dancing," she said at last.

"We are. Afterward."

Afterward meant after he toasted her with Châteauneuf-du-Pape, after an exquisite meal of Caesar salad, crayfish bisque, and swordfish paillard in lemon-caper sauce with sweet peas and pommes duchesse, followed by peach melba and demitasse, and after sitting enthralled at the Majestic Theatre where Dennis had gotten them orchestra seats for *The Phantom of the Opera.*

When they emerged from the crowded theater into the brightly lit street, Roxy noticed women sending admiring glances at him. She tasted the pride of possession as his hand nestled at the small of her back, propelling her to the waiting limo. Rather than returning to the hotel, they drove to Rockefeller Center. He held her hand as an elevator whisked them to the sixty-fifth floor of the GE Building and the Rainbow Room, that elegant cabaret with its spectacular view of the city. Dennis held her close as they danced, his lips brushing her temple. Roxy felt as if she were truly a princess. The only sad note was when he said his trip to California would be coming up soon, and that reminded her that Monday and their separate futures were only hours away.

The thought crystallized on her brain, and impulsively she said, "Dennis, let's go."

Flustered, she hastened to apologize lest he think her ungrateful.

He put a finger to her lips. Attuned to her every nuance, he understood. Her eyes were full of the intoxicating beauty he had come to love. His fingers brushed her cheek. For an instant he forgot they were surrounded by strangers and kissed her. A couple brushed up against them, breaking the spell. Without a word he took her hand and led her off the dance floor.

They fell into each other's arms on the drive to the Plaza, kissing deeply as though starved for reassurance. In their suite they swiftly shed their clothes. Roxy reached for him, pressing her lissome body against his. She came to him with a sense of desperation, with needs she couldn't stem, needs that challenged her cautious philosophy.

Dennis sensed her inner struggle. He wished she could break through her own barriers and recognize love as a freeing, not a confining, emotion. He knew the wounds she carried. What had happened to her sister and the other women she helped wouldn't happen to her, though. Not with him.

She needed time. He would give her that while he showered her with love. . . .

On Monday Dennis sat doodling on a legal pad, his feet propped up on his desk, his tie askew. File folders sat untouched. The only good thing about parting with Roxy earlier that morning was knowing he would see her that evening. He had got her to promise to spend the next four nights at his house, saying it was ridiculous for her to sleep on the floor in a sleeping bag. Before bringing her to his home later, he was going to set up the jungle gym, anchoring it in cement, with John's help.

Pat knocked on his open door and entered at the wave of his hand. She placed a pile of mail on top of the manila folders she had left earlier. Dennis kept on doodling.

She walked back out, shaking her head. "Maggie, you know Roxy Harris. What's she like?"

His office door still open, Dennis heard her. He invited Pat back into his office and told her that Roxy Harris, although not perfect, came close. He then told her to get back to her desk and let him get his work done. Propping his feet back on his desk, he resumed "working" for another hour.

That afternoon he stirred from his lethargy to dictate a letter. He interrupted himself to phone Steven Ostner, inviting him to dinner the following night at seven o'clock.

"Antonia too," Dennis said. "The women can meet."

"What 'women' is that?" Steven asked carefully.

"For a smart man, you're dense. Roxy and Antonia. Who else? I'll stop and pick up Chinese. Roxy likes Chinese food."

Patricia, who knew Dennis didn't care for Chinese food, later told Maggie that Roxy had cast a spell over their boss.


Roxy fared slightly better than Dennis. Each time her mind wandered, she found herself surrounded by people making demands on her time. A reporter for Steven Ostner's statewide newspaper, the *State Press*, called, and she arranged to grant an interview the day of the rally. That gave her and her band of volunteers precious less than a week and a half to prepare.

She furnished the reporter with background information on Safe Havens, which he could print when he announced the rally in his newspaper. When she hung up, she wrote out announcements to send to other newspapers, and also to the local cable network and radio stations.

While preparations for the rally were moving forward, the women at Safe Havens were making strides in getting their lives back together. Allison met with her court-appointed attorney, who had succeeded in garnisheeing her husband's wages. The first check arrived, which meant Allison could pay some overdue bills and take Bettina for a dental checkup. Through Dennis, Shannon phoned and set up meetings with the independent contractor and the insurance adjuster.

As for the rally, Roxy and Nina designated jobs according to skills. Shannon and John were assigned the task of making signs. Allison and Bettina opted to create a flyer for Bob to run off on his laser printer. Maggie said she'd do anything Roxy wanted. In a few days she and Louey would be moving into their new home.

It wasn't until six o'clock that Roxy and Nina found time for a private chat. They relaxed over tea in the office.

"How was your weekend?" Nina asked.

A dreamy look came into Roxy's eyes. "Fabulous. I admit to being infatuated."

Nina shook her head. "So that's what you call it."

"That's what it is." She frowned at Nina, who was wearing one of her I-know-a-secret looks. "Okay, spill it. If you don't, you'll bust." She didn't have long to wait.

"I arranged with the phone company to install call forwarding."

Roxy's cheeks grew warm as a vivid memory of Dennis's body pressed close to hers filled her with a poignant ache. "I'm not going to make a habit of sleeping away from home."

"Regardless, Bob and I insist. We'll work out a

schedule. We should have done it long ago, but we kept hoping you'd switch the late calls to the answering machine. You did over the weekend, and the sky didn't fall down. You should thank Dennis for breaking the cycle. Now you need to learn to ease up a bit more."

"I'm fine," she protested.

Nina leaned forward. "Alice wouldn't want you to be so fixated."

"Stop it. We've been all through this. You're going to say I condemn all men because I hear only about the bad ones. I don't. I'm merely cautious."

"You're overly cautious, Roxy. One of these days it could backfire on you. Now for the good news. A friend of Bob's is updating his office equipment. He'd donating a used computer and fax machine to us."

"You're kidding!" Roxy exclaimed, delighted by their good fortune. "Why didn't you mention this earlier?"

"We were busy," Nina said offhandedly. "And there's more good news."

"More?"

Nina grinned. "I saved the best for last. We're pregnant."

Roxy jumped up and hugged her. She hoped that this time Nina would carry to term. "When is the baby due?"

"Eight and a half months."

Roxy frowned. "Cancel the call forwarding. You need your sleep."

Nina shook her head. "I'm still your partner. That's one of the reasons I ordered it. When you're out during the day, I'll answer the phone."

"Oh, no. Your doctor recommended rest."

"He didn't recommend a coma. I'm not going to be a prisoner. The doctor says I'll need exercise and fresh air. My routine will be light, but I can still work. Bob's going to load duplicate files from here onto our home computer, so I can handle all that work. And after the rally, I want you and Dennis to come for dinner to celebrate. Before you say no, Bob's doing the cooking."

As long as it wouldn't tax her friend's health, Roxy said she'd be happy to celebrate with them. They spoke about the baby and about the precautions Nina would need to take. After Nina left, Roxy said a silent prayer for her friend.

Fate, she mused, thinking of Dennis and the call forwarding Nina and Bob insisted on. Fate was working its hand again, this time in the guise of modern technology.

Dennis arrived at six-thirty. He wore a blue chambray shirt and faded jeans. Roxy barely had time to say hello or to feast her eyes on him as he rushed her into her office and locked the door.

"You," he said accusingly, "made it impossible for me to think straight today. My secretary fears for my sanity. Maggie is half convinced she's working for a simpleminded dolt. My friend Steven Ostner is taking particular delight in my losing my mind. And it's all your fault."

Without giving her a chance to speak, he swept her into his arms and fastened his hungry mouth on hers. His tongue passed the barrier of her lips to tangle greedily with hers while his hands roamed at will.

He lifted his head, breathing heavily. "I spent the better part of the day dreaming of kissing you, and thinking of us last night." He dragged her hand down over the hard bulge in his pants. "See what you do to me," he muttered.

Roxy knew exactly how it felt to be a race-car driver who zoomed from zero to one hundred miles per hour in mere seconds. It had to be their intense physical attraction for each other. Her heart raced. Her knees felt weak. She clung to him, nestling between his thighs. "You're angry," she murmured.

"Desperate is more like it. Until I met you, I knew what the word restraint meant."

Louey banged on the door, calling for Dennis to read him a story. Dennis let out a hiss of breath. "The kid's got lousy timing." He raised his voice. "Give us a few minutes, Louey, then you and John can help me with the jungle gym."

Roxy helplessly shrugged her shoulders. "Privacy is tough to find around here."

"You can say that again. You already know I shuffled papers most of the day. How did your day go?"

"We started to make our plans for the rally. Of course, we're limited."

He perched on the edge of the desk, content for the moment just to look at her. "By what?"

"For one thing, calling all the women on our list ties up the phone. For another, we have no storage space for the signs. But we'll manage. Incidentally, Shannon's making you a sign."

Dennis's expression changed. "Me?"

"You're not reneging, are you?"

"My enthusiasm doesn't match yours, but I'll go. By the way, Steven Ostner's wife, Antonia, wants to meet you. I've invited them for dinner tomorrow night. She and Steven have three kids. She's nice, you'll like her." He slid his hands up her arms. Redheads had extraordinary coloring, he decided. Porcelain and peaches. "What time can we leave?"

"Not before ten."

"Is that the curfew you set for yourself?"

"Please, don't. You're making it hard."

Struggling with impatience, he lost the battle. "Is this the way it's going to be?"

"It's the way it is," Roxy said quietly, searching his face. "I never lied about my priorities. People depend on me."

People, he thought, not one special person. Recognizing an attack of jealousy, he felt rotten. What decent person wouldn't want to help the women and children in need? But it was wrong for Roxy to give up a private life.

"Okay," he said, "But what about tomorrow night? The Ostners are coming to my house at seven."

"Wouldn't it be wiser for them to come here?"

He rubbed the back of a stiffening neck. "Roxy, I invited them to my house, not yours. But even if I hadn't, what about our deal? You see how much privacy we have here—none. They can tour Safe Havens another time. This is a social get-together. Dinner. Two couples. Without interruption. The end of a workday. It wouldn't kill you to relax. You'll be a better, more productive person."

She gazed into his eyes as her fingertips glided across his face. Four promised nights of heaven, she thought. A blink of time in the universe. She couldn't disappoint him or repress her own desires. Giving him a brilliant smile, she leaned toward him. Her lips touched his.

"Before we made love," she whispered, "I said I wanted to be with you. I meant it then; I mean it now. I'll leave early. I'll arrange something."

As his mouth lowered to hers, Dennis couldn't help wondering if negotiating time with Roxy would be the pattern of the future.

# *Eleven*

When Dennis introduced Roxy to Antonia Ostner, it was as if the two women discovered kindred souls or had met in a previous life. There was none of the usual reticence between them, none of the careful stepping-stones that presaged a friendship. Immensely pleased the women hit it off so quickly, Dennis and Steven sat back in their seats at the dining-room table, content to listen to the two sparkling redheads. In contrast to Antonia's cornflower-blue suit, which matched the color of her eyes, Roxy wore a blush-rose linen dress that complemented the rosy tinge of her skin. Delicately wielding chopsticks, the two women talked virtually nonstop throughout Dennis's feast.

He'd bought enough for an army, including wonton soup, Peking duck, sesame beef, triple seafood, sweet-and-sour shrimp, and, for himself, chicken chow mein, the blandest dish on the menu. After the meal, Antonia and Roxy declined the men's offer to help clear the table and sent them to the den to watch baseball.

"Steven's a diehard baseball fan," Antonia said.

"It doesn't matter which team is playing as long as it's baseball."

"It's amazing," Roxy said as she set the teakettle on the burner. "We've just met, yet I feel as if I know you. Dennis was right when he said I'd like you."

Antonia scraped the dishes while Roxy rinsed and put them in the dishwasher. "Steven said the same thing when he came home from the Rotary luncheon. This is a wonderful home. Dennis has good taste, especially in his choice of you."

"We're friends," Roxy clarified quickly. "Good friends, nothing more."

Antonia gave her a careful look. "Are you sure Dennis would agree? He appears to be deeply smitten with you."

"It's infatuation."

Antonia smiled. "That's what I tried to make myself believe with Steven. Thank goodness he knew what I was going through. He had the patience of a saint."

She saw the question in Roxy's eyes that she was too polite to ask and answered it.

"Steven is my second husband. My first husband abused me. If it weren't for a shelter that helps battered women, I wouldn't be here today."

Roxy stared at the woman, who radiated confidence and a strong sense of self-worth. "I would never have guessed," she said.

"There was a time when I thought I'd never be happy again. Certainly, I never thought I'd trust a man again or fall in love and marry, have children. Like other battered women, I had to learn not to blame myself. When Steven mentioned hearing you speak and that you were trying to raise funds for Safe Havens, I wanted to meet you. If Dennis hadn't invited us here tonight, I would have called you."

"I'm so glad a shelter made a difference for you," Roxy said.

"That and the love of a good man. If it weren't for Steven, I wouldn't be as happy as I am today. It's funny how we met. I wanted a new beginning, so I packed up and moved here from Illinois. Since I had worked as a reporter, I applied for a job with Steven's newspaper. Steven told me later he normally doesn't conduct the interviews, but he saw me and decided to interview me."

"And the rest is history."

Antonia smiled in fond memory. "Not quite. Steven decided I need retraining, a lot of it. In the beginning I didn't catch on. Then I did. By that time I was curious. And interested. And scared. Mostly scared. I had sworn not to fall in love, to remain cautious."

Roxy picked up on the word. "You were right about that," she said.

Antonia shook her head as Roxy lifted the whistling kettle from the burner. "No, I wasn't. Steven said he loved me enough for both of us. Thank goodness he didn't give up on me. He's my rock, my strength. We have a wonderful life."

Impulsively, she clasped Roxy's hand. "I hope you'll be as happy with Dennis as I am with Steven. Dennis is a fine man."

Roxy pictured him, her golden heartthrob. Lusty. Loving. Impatient. He could never accept the life she led. She tried to dissuade Antonia from her false notion.

"We're very attracted to each other," she said as she poured the hot water into the teapot, "but I don't have time for a serious relationship. If I did,

I'd first have to know a man for years. Besides, Dennis and I don't have much in common."

Antonia stepped back to study Roxy. "Knowing someone for years doesn't necessarily mean you'll know every facet of his personality. Trust me, I speak from experience. Only marriage, or living together, does that. Am I right in saying Safe Havens is the most important thing in your life?"

"Yes. First it needed every bit of my time to get it started. Now we're so cramped for space, I couldn't forget about it if I tried."

Antonia nodded in understanding. "Even so, I think the real reason you won't commit to Dennis has to do with the morbid stories you hear. Don't let them determine your life."

Roxy looked away, setting out the fortune cookies on a plate. "My sister made a hasty decision to marry. Her husband abused her."

"So that's it," Antonia said as she placed the teapot on a tray. "It's your sister's story that has colored your life. Roxy, if you're unwilling to place faith in Dennis, you'll stay on the outside of happiness. I learned that with Steven's help. If you're in love, you owe it to yourself to grab your share of personal joy."

Roxy put the plate of cookies on the tray. "You sound like my parents and my partner."

"That should tell you something. The tea's ready. Let's call the men."

Antonia's statements pricked at Roxy's conscience. Exactly how deeply did she feel about Dennis? Hearing Antonia's call, the men drifted into the kitchen. Dennis looped his arm around Roxy's shoulders, then they all went into the dining room where Roxy poured the tea.

She told Antonia about the rally and thanked Steven for the interview with his paper. Steven and his wife thought the rally was a splendid idea.

"We're going to use my house as a command post."

All heads swiveled toward Dennis, who had made the comment.

"Command post?" Roxy repeated. This was news to her. From the first Dennis had been lukewarm to her idea.

It was news to Dennis too. The words had simply popped out of his mouth. Why he didn't know, but if fate had made him blurt that out, the reason had to be to keep Roxy with him for as long as he could.

"Command post," he reiterated, praying fate would now complete the explanation.

Roxy, bless her heart, nodded in understanding. "What Dennis means," she said to the Ostners, "is that since this house is so much larger than mine, he's offering it for our worthy cause. Space is a problem at my place. Also, if we tie up the phone soliciting help for the rally, we prevent important calls from coming in. We need to keep on top of things in a central location. It's quite an undertaking on such short notice. Thank you, darling." She reached for Dennis's hand.

He beamed. "Darling" sounded wonderful on her lips. If they were alone, she'd be in his arms right now. Thinking of kissing her luscious body, he wished his guests would leave immediately.

Roxy patted his hand, then went on with growing fervor. "It'll be like a commanding general's headquarters. Why the women, children, and the band can assemble here before we board the buses! We'll ask the reporters to conduct their interviews from here."

Dennis stopped beaming. Stopped fantasizing. He pictured hordes of people descending on his home, invading his privacy. Preventing him from being alone with Roxy!

"Buses?" he repeated. "Reporters? Why can't everyone meet at city hall?"

"They can, darling. But think how much better it will be if you first give everyone a pep talk. You can give it on the individual buses, so your neighbors won't be bothered by people trampling their lawns."

Dennis squirmed. "Why me? I don't give pep talks. I told you I've never even been to a political rally."

"Darling, this is different. You believe in our cause, and you're a man." She leaned over to kiss his cheek. "You're decent, honest, and you're committed to our cause. Of course you. I can't think of a better role model for the children. Not after seeing you with Maggie's and Shannon's kids. He was wonderful, Antonia."

Hearing Roxy make him into a hero brought a thin smile to Dennis's lips.

"My evenings are going to be very busy," Roxy said, "making certain the preparations for the rally go smoothly."

"You'll do that from here, naturally," Dennis said.

"Of course. What's a command post for?"

Antonia suggested Roxy contact workers at other shelters, state agencies, and private counselors. "Invite everyone as long as you're at it."

Steven offered to ask his colleagues at the other newspapers to send reporters. "Dennis, you know people at the radio station and the local TV. Call them."

Roxy was thrilled. "I did send announcements, but, darling, if you know a reporter who can come to cover the rally for television, that's even better.

A picture is worth a thousand words. We'll keep up the momentum, maintain public awareness. We could go on TV, even start a radiothon." She pounced on still another idea. "We'll announce my next activity from here. Right on your porch steps."

Dennis tried not to blanch. One look at Roxy's glowing face and he knew he had opened a Pandora's box.

She caught his expression, and her own became suspicious. "That is what you meant by a command post, isn't it, darling?"

No, it wasn't! His concept of a command post—if he had to define one—would be limited to exclusivity. His and hers. His palms began to sweat. He wanted Roxy in his bed, in his arms, for longer than this week, so he could convince her they were made for each other. He wanted her to go to California with him. He had a gift for her, a sheer sexy nightgown that had caught his eye in the window of a lingerie store. He saw himself slowly kissing it off her.

So, no. Not by the wildest stretch of his imagination would his command post include a barrage of reporters, TV hounds with miles of cable wire, buses parked at his curb, or himself serving up speeches to a battalion of strangers.

For Roxy's cause he'd much rather rent tents in a big field and let someone else pep up the crowd!

He couldn't say that, though, for two reasons. One: Even to himself he sounded like Scrooge, and he didn't like that. Two: Hearing Roxy repeatedly call him "darling" was music to his ears. He didn't want her to stop. He picked up her hand and kissed her palm.

"It's exactly what I meant," he said.

Steven and Antonia were watching him. He

caught their amused stares. When they started to speak, his glower silenced them; then he sent a devastating smile in Roxy's direction.

"Tell me, sweet, what activity were you thinking of next?"

The words came out on a burst of inspiration. "It has to be something different," she said. "Something to pull at the imagination. I know!" She smiled at him. "I'll jump."

Dennis gaped at her in horror. "As in parachute out of an airplane?"

She nodded. "It's a great idea, darling."

He scowled, cursing his big mouth. "It's an awful idea. Suppose you get hurt? I won't have it, Roxy. You'll give me gray hairs. How could you even think of that?"

"I'll be perfectly safe. It's a great fund-raising idea, darling. We can sell raffle tickets."

"No way!" His voice thundered. His fist hit the table. "You know how I feel about you falling out of airplanes."

Roxy smiled benignly at the Ostners as she patted Dennis's hand. "Dennis is a worrywart. Please don't think it makes him less of a man. He's really very brave."

The Ostners solemnly swore the thought would never cross their minds.

Dennis groaned.

"Now then," Roxy blithely continued, "we'll have people guess where I'll land. I'll jump several times. Otherwise it's unfair for people to drive all the way to the field. Dennis, do you know any merchants who might be willing to donate prizes?"

Sure as shooting, he thought, the little minx was suckering him in.

"I'll see," he muttered.

She smiled. "I told you he was wonderful," she said to the Ostners. "Who better than Dennis to let the world know what an accomplished skydiver I am? We met thanks to wind shear."

She turned her beatific smile on Dennis. "All this is thanks to you, darling, for donating your lovely home as a command post."

For two cents he'd put a For Sale sign on the property in the morning.

"What do you think of my plans, Antonia?" Roxy asked.

Antonia covered her mouth to hide her grin. "They make perfect sense to me."

"And don't forget, Roxy," Dennis said, determined to hang on to his one trump card, "you did say you'd spend your nights here so I can be of greater assistance. Just until the rally is over, of course."

"Of course," she said. How bad could it be, Dennis thought, to give a couple of pep talks when the rewards were so great? He let the conversation swirl around him, smiling each time Roxy called him "darling." He knew he wasn't going to do anything foolish, like confess to her his reason for offering his house. He'd get around to his mea culpa in due time. After Roxy fell in love with him. Women in love forgave more easily.

When the Ostners were ready to leave, Steven took him aside while Antonia cleared the table with Roxy. He pumped Dennis's hand.

"What's that for?" Dennis asked.

"For meeting your match. Roxy's quite a woman."

In the kitchen Antonia said she wanted to donate food. "People will be hungry later."

Roxy thanked her. "With Dennis's help Safe Havens can't miss." She bit her bottom lip and suddenly broke out laughing. "Poor man. What I put him through."

Antonia's jaw dropped, then she started to laugh too. "You knew why he offered his house, didn't you?"

"Of course I did. The man's desperate to keep me here."

"What are you going to do?"

Roxy wiped her eyes. When she stopped laughing, she said, "After you leave, I'm going to show him my sincere appreciation."

Antonia collapsed with mirth. "Terrific. You both win."

Dennis and Roxy strolled into the den. They sat down together on the couch, and she snuggled against him. Tilting her head back, she gazed into his eyes.

"Thank you for all you're doing. It means more than I can say."

He felt her smile clear to his toes. His undeserving-of-her-gratefulness toes. Recrimination sliced through him.

She kissed the pulse at his neck. "Darling, your heart's racing."

Deep inside his gut he knew confession time was at hand. His body would betray him if he tried to make love to her with a guilty conscience. If he didn't love her, he could take her to bed. Now that he loved her, he couldn't.

*Fate, you've sure got funny ways.*

"Sit down, sweetheart," he said.

"I am sitting."

Frowning, he looked into her wide, smoldering green eyes. Her honest green eyes. He memorized how she looked when she was calm. It might have to last him a long time. "You're gorgeous."

"Thank you. Why are you frowning?"

He rubbed the back of his neck. "Sorry. I didn't know that I was." Easing away from her, he rose to pace the den.

"Dennis, why are you pacing?"

He stopped.

"You're acting strange. Is it about offering your house?"

He let out a deep breath. "Roxy, do you know why I did?"

She smiled and let out a long, dreamy sigh. "Yes. You're generous, kind, wonderful, and marvelous."

His confession shriveled. "Besides that."

She folded her hands in her lap. "To help me?"

"That's not exactly the entire reason."

She brushed an imaginary speck of lint from her arm. "To relax me?"

He cocked his head. "You're getting close."

She looked him square in the eyes. "To relax yourself."

His head tipped down. "Explain that."

"You know."

"If I did, I wouldn't ask."

She wrung her hands. Her lips trembled. Her shoulders shook. He rushed to her, squatting on his haunches and grabbing her hands, determined to wipe away the sadness that had suddenly engulfed her. "Sweetheart, don't be upset."

Roxy couldn't contain herself. She burst into laughter. "Dennis, you're a rotten actor. You should have seen the look on your face when you offered your home as a command post. As though my ladies are part of an army." She hooted. "You pulled that out of the hat to get me to sleep with you for more than four days."

He threw down her hands. "You little devil! You knew," he cried. "Why didn't you say something?"

"I wanted to see how far you'd go."

"You cheated."

She tossed her head. "How is it worse than what you tried to do?"

"If I had asked you without it, would you have consented to stay?"

She saw the serious look in his eye. "I'm not sure. Maybe. You've agreed to do so much to help us."

He frowned. "Roxy, I don't want you as part of a barter."

"I know. I'm sorry for saying that. Why did you tell me the truth?"

"Don't you know? Can't you guess? I haven't been myself since we met. I suppose by offering my home I showed how desperate I am."

She saw the pain in his eyes. Suddenly, the game she had played seemed shallow, undeserving. "Put your arms around me, Dennis. Talk to me."

His feelings came out in a rush. "Roxy, you're too gung ho. You attack from all sides. I flat-out refuse to watch you jump. I wasn't kidding when I said I'll turn gray. I'll have a heart attack. If you think I'm a coward, I can't help it."

"Could you watch another person jump?" she asked softly, her heart overflowing.

His lips touched her cheek. "Of course."

"Why, darling?"

He shuddered. As if the words were dragged from the depths of his being, he said, "I'm in love with you, Roxy."

Her heart took a little leap. Waves of exquisite tenderness flowed through her.

But Dennis saw the wariness in her eyes and sighed. He knew she hadn't wanted to hear that. He'd said it too soon. Still, he couldn't keep his hands from sliding down her back to draw her closer. "Forget I said that, but you did ask for my reason. I know you think we have nothing in common. I just want the time to prove you wrong."

She kissed him softly. In that moment when he looked so genuinely miserable and woebegone, all her stalwart decisions not to fall in love with him fled. Every fiber of her being reached out to him. She loved him. As much as she feared to face that fact, she loved him. As much as she masked her love by saying she was infatuated, she loved him.

She soothed his forehead. "We're very well suited sexually."

He recalled their passion-filled nights. Now, with her in his arms and trailing her lips over his chin, his neck, he was hard and growing harder.

"Dennis," she murmured, her lips at the pulse in his neck. "Would it help if I told you I loved you too?"

He was deathly afraid he was hallucinating, that he'd heard only what he wanted to hear. He held her back from him, studying her face.

"You're not just saying that to make me feel better, are you? Or do you mean you love me like a friend?"

Roxy saw the hope, the question behind the simmering happiness in his silvery eyes. She smiled a slow, sexy smile. "Hardly. I'm as surprised as you are."

Disbelief gave way to wonderment and the stunning realization of his good fortune. "I love you." He hugged her to him, celebrating her gift with a kiss that left her toes curling. And his. He buried his face in her hair, nuzzling her neck to breathe in her fragrance.

"I didn't intend to fall in love with you," she murmured. "I much prefer infatuation."

"Why?"

She eased back to look at him, letting him see the residue of fear within her. "Infatuations end. They're safer."

He smiled in sham sympathy. "I'm irresistible, and you just couldn't help yourself. Is that it?"

She laid her head on his chest. "Mmmm, true. You came along at a very inappropriate time."

"Don't let it bother you."

He skimmed his fingertips along the delicate line of her jaw, then lifted her chin. As his lips touched hers, Roxy began to feel light-headed, intoxicated. She pulled his head down to increase the pressure.

"Nina's pregnant," she murmured against his mouth. "I'm going to be busier than ever until I get help."

Dennis gazed down at her smiling. Help or no help, his bright, determined Roxy would always be busy. It was her nature. Just as it was his duty to offer her balance in her life.

His eyes twinkled. "Do you agree I'm an expert in time management?"

She nodded.

"Then why don't we finish this conversation in bed?"

"Is there more magic dust?"

His hands whispered across her skin, already sprinkling some on her. "I have it on reliable information that there is."

She linked her fingers through his. "Then by all means, let's continue this conversation upstairs."

# *Twelve*

The morning of the rally Dennis awakened with his arms wound around Roxy; by now it was a familiar embrace. Sex was better when you were in love, he decided. It was more meaningful. He still couldn't get over his miracle, for that was how he thought of his fiery angel. He relished everything about her. Her enthusiasm. Her kindness. Her commitment to people.

Roxy had contacted a real estate agent in Shannon's old neighborhood, asking about rentals. The children missed their friends. His own contacts had assured him that Shannon would get the insurance checks to cover her losses. While it would take time to get her life together, Shannon's spirits had lifted. She could see light at the end of the tunnel.

His best personal news was wrangling a promise from Roxy to abandon her crazy idea of selling raffle tickets to watch her skydive. She made that promise after several of his clients pledged a monthly sum to Safe Havens.

Life would never be dull with her. He loved the way she tingled with excitement when she heard good news, but he especially loved to see her eyes deepen in color when they made love. Without question, he adored her.

Except for one thing.

She stubbornly avoided talking about marriage and setting a wedding date.

"We have to get to know each other better first," she'd said the first time he'd proposed, a week earlier.

"How much more do we need to know about?" he demanded.

"I'm not sure." She kissed his mouth and pressed her body to his, and after that he forgot everything.

The next time he'd broached the subject, four days ago, she was sitting in his bathtub, her arms wrapped around her knees. Her skin had a rosy hue, and though she'd piled her hair atop her head, curly tendrils had come free, framing her face. Her eyes were closed, and she was humming along with a song on the radio. He switched it off and asked.

"Darling, let's not rush," she said. "We'll know when we're ready." Then she held her arms out, beckoning him to join her.

He'd decided last night that after the rally, he would ask her one more time and not be put off. This time she would set a date. She had his heart, his future. Without her he would be an empty shell. She brought life and joy to his home. Their home, he thought, gazing down at her. A home that one day would ring with the sound of their children.

And not, he thought, rolling his eyes, with the chaos he was certain to witness that day. Signs were stacked on his front porch and covered with plastic sheeting, ready to be loaded onto the buses. He had contracted for two of them, each holding fifty-four people. A wealthy client had paid that bill.

Thanks to television news bites, the *State Press*,

and other newspapers, word of the rally to help battered and abused women and children had spread like wildfire. Roxy, herself, had been a whirlwind for two weeks, attending to her regular day's work and then toiling on her campaign at night. Dennis's only bright spot was that all those nights had been spent with him.

Roxy snuggled closer to Dennis. She had been awake for several minutes, counting her blessings. Since he had allowed her and her ladies to use his home, he had become their overnight champion. He couldn't do enough for them and often anticipated their needs. He'd even distributed flyers to the local merchants to display in their windows. He was a wonderful, wonderful man.

She touched her lips to his chest, letting him know she was awake.

"Today's the day," she whispered excitedly. "I hope we'll hit it lucky. Maybe someone will donate a small building or a large house. Then Safe Havens can offer more services."

Dennis said nothing for a minute. To think, he mused, he was wishing she'd set a wedding date. She was wishing for more work. Telling himself to be patient, he lifted her hand to his lips and kissed it.

"It's going to be a beautiful day for the rally." He paused and looked directly into her eyes. "I'm going to miss you when I leave for California on Monday. Come with me. I'll be called to testify only once or twice at the most. We can go to Disneyland, tour the movie studios, take a side trip to Vegas. We can both use a vacation."

She propped herself on the pillows. "I wish I could go. It sounds fabulous. But Nina's working at home already, and I'm trying to find someone to help me. This isn't a good time."

She tried placating him with a kiss, but Dennis

wasn't placated. He had to face his growing fear that he was chasing an elusive dream. Roxy was generous and passionate. She loved without restraint. She praised him, fussed over him, teased him. She did so many things to please him, yet he was beginning to wonder if she would ever make the commitment to get married. Her future revolved around Safe Havens. His revolved around her.

"What about Antonia?" he asked. "She wants to help."

Roxy wished with all her heart she could tell Dennis what he wanted to hear, but she couldn't. Even thinking about getting married gave her the jitters. If she told him that, he'd think she didn't love him, and she did. Or he would tell her in his logical way that many women and men had similar trepidations. Marriage was a big step. How well she knew. She listened to enough stories about the breakups of marriages to fill volumes. Still, she supposed Dennis was right. Many people married successfully. And many did get cold feet. However, it usually occurred right before the wedding ceremony, not right after declaring your love for a man.

"What about Antonia?" Dennis repeated, watching her. "I'm sure she'll agree if it's for a week."

Roxy shook her head. "I can't leave an untrained person. It wouldn't be fair."

He could feel his shoulder blades tighten. Throwing off the covers, he got out of bed. Every damn one of her replies made good sense, yet each carried the same underlying message. "I love you, but . . ."

He turned to face her. She'd sat up, her arms wrapped protectively around her knees.

"Roxy, do you want to marry me?"

"Dennis, please. I love you. Don't rush me."

His lips thinned. "Okay. Let me know when you

make up your mind about getting married, Roxy. I'm getting tired of sounding like a broken record."

Roxy winced. She deserved that. But she had nothing to say as he stalked out of the room.

Even though Roxy and Dennis were strained with each other at first, the rally was a huge success. All of Roxy's former guests who lived in the area showed up to lend support. Many brought their children. Workers from various state agencies and other shelters came. Before the buses left for city hall, Dennis kept his promise to give pep talks. The buses quickly filled up, and more people met them near city hall. Labor groups and women's groups sent delegations from the surrounding areas and from neighboring states. The press treated Roxy like a feminine version of David taking on Goliath.

During her short speech she made clear the number of women and children who needed help, and how little aid was available. Without insulting the mayor or the other politicians who were there, she asked them specific questions and challenged them to announce definitely when additional funding would be allocated to help battered women.

Afterward many returned to Dennis's house, where Antonia provided sandwiches and drinks. Finally, everyone left except for Bill Halliday, a fifteen-year veteran reporter for Steven Ostner's paper.

With her shoes off, her legs curled to the side, Roxy sat nestled against Dennis on the couch in his den, answering Bill's questions.

"All right," he said at the end of the interview, "I have all I need about Safe Havens, but the article will read better if I add a few personal facts."

"I know," she said. "Steven mentioned that the

other night. What sort of information are you looking for?"

His glance went briefly to Dennis's arm, wrapped possessively around her shoulders. "Anything. Your training. If you have a hobby."

She brightened. "I skydive."

"Not for long," Dennis said. "Not if I have anything to say about it."

She squeezed his hand. "He worries needlessly."

Bill smiled. "I wouldn't want my wife jumping out of planes either."

"Oh, we're not married," Roxy said.

"Engaged?" the reporter asked.

"Friends."

Dennis looked at her meaningfully.

"Good friends," she amended, patting his knee.

Bill closed his notebook. "My mistake. I thought you two . . ." He shrugged. He thanked her and shook hands, then Dennis walked him to the door.

Dennis took his time returning to the den. The force of public rejection gathered within him until he couldn't stand the fire in his gut. Roxy was a first-class coward. No wonder she wouldn't set a wedding date. She couldn't even bring herself to say she was in love, let alone about to be formally engaged. He clenched his jaw as he stood in the doorway. He saw the distress on her face, but it was too late. She had closed the door on their future.

"Dennis," she began, starting across the room to him, "I couldn't tell him—"

"Forget it!" Her eyes widened in shock at his cold tone. "You answered both our questions at the same time." He went to the phone and dialed a number.

Roxy gave a quick involuntary shudder. His eyes were fixed on her as if he were seeing her for the first time, seeing a woman he couldn't stand. "What are you doing?"

"I'm calling you a cab."

"Nina and Bob are expecting us."

"Give them my apologies. I'm not in a party mood. Get your things. The cab will be here in a few minutes."

The blood drained out of her face as the enormity of his hurt crashed down upon her. She squeezed shut her eyes. "I love you."

He made a guttural sound. She couldn't begin to know how much he loved her, he thought. Even now he wanted to touch her so badly, to kiss her senseless, but he knew it wouldn't work. Not if he waited a lifetime. Better to cut his wrists and bleed fast.

"Roxy, you don't have the foggiest idea what love means. Not with me, at any rate. You're Miss Noble, out to save the world. Groups, Roxy. All deserving, I grant you, but nevertheless groups. Safety in numbers. I'm okay to satisfy a bodily urge. You've gotten used to that, but more? Oh, no. Saying you love me doesn't carry commitment. The only thing you're committed to is Safe Havens. And do you know why? No one is permanent there. Everyone is passing through. You're safe. There's no man to threaten the shell you crawl into every time you go up to your attic bedroom alone. I want more, and one day I'll find a woman who's not a coward. When I do, she sure as hell won't mix me up with her brother-in-law or any other man. She'll see me for who I am. Love me for who I am."

Tears were flowing down her face. He left her alone to wait for the cab.

• • •

Roxy lay on the bed in her attic room. She had wept until there were no more tears, worked until she was ready to drop from exhaustion, then repeated the routine the following day. Three weeks had passed since she had caused the breakup with Dennis. She'd lost weight. Grim lines of fatigue were her constant companion.

In his article, Bill Halliday called her a heroine. Nina called her a dope. Roxy had run out of names to call herself.

She had chosen her single destiny, exiled herself from life. Now she had time, all the time in the world, and she had never been so unhappy. Her caution had brought her misery. Late at night when she listened to the house creaking, when her hand reached out to the empty pillow next to her head, she told herself it was for the best.

Still, work lost its appeal. She dragged through her days. Safe Havens flourished, nonetheless. People pledged money. She hired an aide, Florence Newsom, and she took a load off her shoulders. That left Roxy with more time to mope. A real estate company had offered to donate a small, unoccupied apartment building to Safe Havens. She and the Arnouths were in the process of working out the necessary details. Roxy switched on the answering machine every night, using it so she could escape to her private agonies. She spent more hours outside the house, whether it was testifying to help make new laws, or canvassing for jobs for women, or other duties. And the sky, as Nina said, hadn't fallen down.

Only on her. Her life had collapsed around her.

Visiting Nina one afternoon, she tried to put on

a good front, telling her friend that Dennis was wrong for her.

Nina handed her a tissue. "You're right there, kiddo. Why be happy when you can be miserable? Now take Bob and me. We're stupid. We got married, and we're dumb enough to enjoy sleeping together, making love, talking about this and that, and sometimes even fighting."

Roxy smiled wanly. "You made your point."

"Are you going to see Dennis? He's back from California, you know."

Roxy shook her head. "No."

She didn't tell Nina she had seen Dennis coming out of a fashionable restaurant just the day before. He'd been with a stunning blond woman, his arm was wrapped familiarly around her shoulders. Before opening the door to his car, he'd drawn the woman to him for a kiss on the cheek.

He'd glanced up a moment later and saw Roxy. Neither had moved, as if they were frozen in a stop-action film. Roxy had only prayed her eyes didn't look as wounded as she felt. Responding to a call from his date, he'd gotten into the car and sped away.

It was obvious he had wasted no time in finding a replacement.

Still pained by that, she stood to leave.

"You've only been here a few minutes," Nina said. She looked worried.

"I'm sorry. I'm not very good company. I wanted to see you, to let you know everything is going well at Safe Havens."

Nina begged her to stay. "How are you making out with the books? Are you using Dennis's system?"

"Florence is."

"What are you doing this weekend?"

She shrugged. "Going to Alexandria Field, I guess. I haven't been skydiving for a while. Tell Bob I'll meet him there Sunday morning at nine."

She hadn't felt much like doing anything for the past three weeks. She woke up listless, went to bed listless. She had started taking vitamins to give her pep. So far, they hadn't worked.

Dennis's accusation plagued her. For the first time she faced herself with brutal honesty. He was right. She did use what had happened to Alice and the other battered women as a shield against personal relationships, terrified that she might choose the wrong man. Instead, she threw away the only man for her. Dennis knew there were no guarantees. He wasn't afraid to face life. The blonde was lucky. She would know the love of the best man in the world. The tears threatening to overflow again, Roxy said good-bye to Nina.

The blue Cessna leveled off at ten thousand feet. Roxy waited for Bob Arnouth's signal. Tapping her shoulder, he shouted above the roar of the plane's engines, "Remember to check your altimeter speed and pull the rip cord at three thousand feet. Have a good ride. Go!"

She stepped outward, reveling in the sensation of tumbling in space, a brightly plumed bird in yellow coveralls, with a white helmet. Arms and legs spread wide, and with no cloud cover to obscure her vision, she rotated her body to see the vistas below. Rooftops, church steeples, buildings, homes, and cars grew larger as she flew downward.

The noiseless air caressed her face, brushed her clothes. The freefall had always been her favorite part of the jump. Today it meant nothing. Just a jump, a fall through space. Like the rest of her life.

At three thousand feet she yanked the rip cord and counted. In three seconds a 220-square-foot canopy of red-and-white nylon unfurled, tugging her gently to an upright position. Peering at the ground, she continued flying downward. Suddenly, she couldn't believe what she was seeing. A man, his arms outstretched, his hands cupped as if ready to catch a ball, zigged and zagged across the field, heading toward her. She glanced around. There was no one else around. But it couldn't be happening twice! Then she got a good look at him and let out a war whoop.

Dennis's heart leaped into his throat. He ran as if he were jet-propelled, changing course slightly to sprint out of the sun's blinding rays. She was coming down fast, kicking her feet, sending him a frantic message.

He powered down, picking up more speed until he neared her projected landing site. His brain whirled. He still didn't trust the damn chute. He never would. Calm, he told himself. First and foremost he had to keep himself calm.

Above him, her whole self a riot of hopeful anticipation, Roxy felt as if her heart had skipped into the stratosphere.

"I'm coming!" she yelled.

Dennis, bless him, grew larger by the second. The Man Upstairs was giving her a second chance. He had to be. Why else would Dennis be there? To tell her he didn't want her? He had already done that. It could only mean he had changed his mind.

She hoped.

"I've got you," he called up to her. "Don't worry

about me, angel. You're safe. I saw everything. I'll save you."

"Dennis," she wailed, "you don't have to go through the entire thing again. I love you. I want to marry you."

"Is that a proposal?" he yelled.

She was nearly down. A few more seconds. "Darling, get out of the way, or we'll both land in the hospital! I want your children."

"Are you asking me to marry you?"

She hit the ground running and quickly stopped herself. Dennis was right there, and she threw herself at him.

He grabbed her arms, though, and held her away from him. "Did I hear you correctly?"

"Yes." Her mouth covered his. She felt him relax as she kissed him over and over. "Yes. Yes. Yes."

The expression in his eyes softened. "Call me 'darling.'"

"Darling. I love you. I want babies."

"Don't worry, I'll give them to you. Right now, if you keep this up."

Grinning, she unhooked her rig. "What are you doing here?"

"When I saw how unhappy you looked the other day, it gave me the courage to try to convince you not to throw our future away. When I couldn't get you at home, I phoned Nina."

Roxy reared back, a dangerous glint in her eye. "You didn't look miserable the other day. Who was that blonde I saw you with, hotshot?"

He smiled. "That's how I knew you couldn't live without me. You were jealous! You said you don't want me to make any other woman feel the way I make you feel, right?"

"Who was she, Jorden?"

"Not so fast. Before I let you have your way with

me, there are a few things we have to settle, Roxy."

Her hands landed on her hips. "Who was she, Jorden?"

He scooped up handfuls of her parachute. "Do you plan on keeping regular working hours?"

She advanced on him. "Yes. Who was she, Jorden?"

He stepped out of her reach. "How many kids do you want?"

She shrugged. "Three. Four. Five. Eight."

He grinned. "Great tax deductions. I assume you won't skydive while pregnant."

"Of course not. I wouldn't put my babies' lives in jeopardy."

"Nine kids then." He stopped her from grabbing the parachute from him by pressing a kiss to her mouth. Liking the sample so much, he lingered for more.

"We live in my house," he murmured against her mouth.

"Our house." She pulled her head back. "But the hot tub's mine. Who was she, Jorden?"

He chucked her under the chin. "My sister, Jennifer. She came in from Norfolk with her husband. I was taking her to lunch."

She threw her arms around Dennis's neck and helped herself to a scorching kiss.

At last they came up for air. "Does this mean I get to share the hot tub with you?" he asked.

Loving him, laughing and kissing him at the same time, she hugged him tight. "That, and everything else, darling."

He grinned. "Say it again."

She did. Over and over and over . . .

# THE EDITOR'S CORNER

There's a kind of hero we all love, the kind who usually wears irresistible tight jeans and holds a less-than-glamorous job. The world doesn't always sing his praises, but the world couldn't do without him—and next month LOVESWEPT salutes him with **MEN AT WORK**. In six fabulous new romances that feature only these men on the covers, you'll meet six heroes who are unique in many ways, yet are all hardworking, hard-driving, and oh, so easy to love!

First, let Billie Green sweep you away to Ireland, where you'll meet a hunk of a sheep farmer, Keith Donegal. He's the **MAN FROM THE MIST,** LOVESWEPT #564, and Jenna Howard wonders if his irresistible heat is just a spell woven by the land of leprechauns. But with dazzling kisses and thrilling caresses, Keith sets out to prove that the fire between them is the real thing. The magic of Billie's writing shines through in this enchanting tale of love and desire.

In **BUILT TO LAST** by Lori Copeland, LOVESWEPT #565, the hero, Bear Malone, is exactly what you would expect from his name—big, eye-catching, completely fascinating, and with a heart to match his size. A carpenter, he renovates houses for poor families, and he admires the feisty beauty Christine Brighton for volunteering for the job. Now, if he can only convince her that they should make a home and a family of their own . . . Lori makes a delightful and sensual adventure out of building a house.

You'll get plenty of **MISCHIEF AND MAGIC** in Patt Bucheister's new LOVESWEPT, #566. Construction worker Phoenix Sierra knows all about mischief from his friends' practical jokes, and when he lands in an emergency room because of one, he finds magic in Deborah Justin. The copper-haired doctor is enticing, but before she will love Phoenix, he must reveal the vulnerable man hiding behind his playboy facade. You'll keep turning the pages as Patt skillfully weaves this tale of humor and passion.

Kimberli Wagner returns to LOVESWEPT with **A COWBOY'S TOUCH,** LOVESWEPT #567, and as before, she is sure to enchant you with her provocative writing and ability to create sizzling tension. In this story, Jackie Stone ends up working as the cook on her ex-husband's ranch because she desperately needs the money. But Gray Burton has learned from his mistakes, and he'll use a cowboy's touch to persuade Jackie to return to his loving arms. Welcome back, Kim!

There can't be a more perfect—or sexy—title for a book in which the hero is an electric lineman than **DANGEROUS IN THE DARK** by Terry Lawrence, LOVESWEPT #568. Zach Young is a lineman for the county, the one to call when the lights go out. When he gets caught in an electric storm, he finds shelter in Candy Wharton's isolated farmhouse. He makes Candy feel safe in the dark; the danger is in allowing him into her heart. All the stirring emotions that you've come to expect from Terry are in this fabulous story.

Olivia Rupprecht gives us a memorable gift of love with **SAINTS AND SINNERS,** LOVESWEPT #569. Matthew

Peters might be a minister, but he's no saint—and he's determined to get to know gorgeous Delilah Sampson, who's just moved in across the street from his Iowa church. He's as mortal as the next man, and he can't ignore a woman who's obviously in trouble . . . or deny himself a taste of fierce passion. Once again, Olivia delivers an enthralling, powerful romance.

On sale this month from FANFARE are four breathtaking novels. **A WHOLE NEW LIGHT** proves why Sandra Brown is a *New York Times* bestselling author. In this story, widow Cyn McCall wants to shake up her humdrum life, but when Worth Lansing asks her to spend a weekend with him in Acapulco, she's more than a little surprised—and tempted. Worth had always been her friend, her late husband's business partner. What will happen when she sees him in a whole new light?

Award-winning author Rosanne Bittner sets **THUNDER ON THE PLAINS** in one of America's greatest eras—the joining of the East and West by the first transcontinental railroad. Sunny Landers is the privileged daughter of a powerful railroad magnate. Colt Travis is the half-Indian scout who opens her eyes to the beauty and danger of the West . . . and opens her heart to love.

**INTIMATE STRANGERS** is a gripping and romantic time-travel novel by Alexandra Thorne. On vacation in Santa Fe, novelist Jane Howard slips into a flame-colored dress and finds herself transported to 1929, in another woman's life, in her home . . . and with her husband.

Critically acclaimed author Patricia Potter creates a thrilling historical romance with **LIGHTNING**. During the Civil War, nobody was a better blockade runner for the South than Englishman Adrian Cabot, but Lauren Bradly swore to stop him. Together they would be swept into passion's treacherous sea, tasting deeply of ecstasy and the danger of war.

Also on sale this month, in the hardcover edition from Doubleday, is **SINFUL** by Susan Johnson. Sweeping from the majestic manors of England to the forbidden salons of a Tunisian harem, this is a tale of desperate deception and sensual pleasures between a daring woman and a passionate nobleman.

Happy reading!

With best wishes,

*Nita Taublib*

Nita Taublib
Associate Publisher
LOVESWEPT and FANFARE

Don't miss these fabulous Bantam Fanfare titles
on sale in JULY.

# A WHOLE NEW LIGHT
by Sandra Brown

# THUNDER ON THE PLAINS
by Rosanne Bittner

# INTIMATE STRANGERS
by Alexandra Thorne

# LIGHTNING
by Patricia Potter

And in hardcover from Doubleday,
# SINFUL
by Susan Johnson

# A WHOLE NEW LIGHT

by

*New York Times* bestselling author

**Sandra Brown**

Cyn McCall knew she could always count on her late husband's friend and business partner, Worth Lansing. He could always make her laugh and forget her problems—she could tease him about his many romantic entanglements. The last thing Cyn expected was to lose herself in longing for a man who could never settle down.

When Worth invited his best friend Cyn to a getaway weekend in Acapulco he never suspected that he'd respond to her the way he did to any beautiful woman. While he thought it was time she stopped mourning and moved forward with her life, he couldn't escape the feeling he was betraying Tim's memory. But guilt couldn't stop the rising tide of desire threatening to overwhelm him.

Cyn wanted to believe that their night of abandon was sparked by the exotic locale and intoxicating scent of hibiscus. Worth knew they shared something deeper, a passion that would outlast the Mexican sunglow . . . if only Cyn would open her heart to new possibilities and the promise of love.

# THUNDER ON THE PLAINS

by

Rosanne Bittner

bestselling author of

IN THE SHADOW OF THE MOUNTAINS

*It was a time of enormous turmoil and far-reaching expansion for America. The Civil War and the assassination of a President had torn the nation apart, but one man's great vision—of building a transcontinental railroad that would join the East and West could reunite it. Bo Landers's lifelong wish became his daughter's destiny.*

*Sunny Landers was utterly devoted to her father's dream . . . until she met Colt Travis. And she knew, with the searing shock of a lightning bolt, that he was the only man she could ever love, though their worlds might separate them.*

*Half Cherokee, but raised by whites, Colt Travis was like the vast, rugged land of his birth: handsome to gaze upon, yet wild, imposing, and dangerous. When he first laid eyes on the spirited, passionate daughter of Bo Landers, the man who'd hired him to scout into the Western territories, he knew she was everything he'd ever want in a woman . . . but believed he could never have.*

"It's getting almost too hot," Colt told Sunny. "You sure you don't want to go back?"

"No. Not yet."

"Just be careful you don't let the sun burn that pretty face."

She laughed lightly, lifting the canteen and drinking some more water. She offered it to him, and Colt met her eyes. He swore if he didn't know her better, she was giving him a look of invitation, but he was not about to take that road. It could lead to nowhere but disaster for both of them. What in God's name was this all about?

The woman was to be married soon! What the hell was he doing out here in no-man's land, riding with the richest woman in the country, a woman who dined with presidents and owned half of Chicago and dished out millions like pennies, a woman who was part owner of the very company for which he worked? This was the most absurd situation he had ever encountered! He took a swallow of water and handed back the canteen, then reached behind him to get out tobacco and a cigarette paper.

"That's the scar from when you were wounded by the Pawnee, isn't it?" she asked, her eyes resting at his right side.

Colt rolled himself a cigarette. "It is. I've finally managed to put all that behind me."

She began undoing her braid. "Where do you go from here, Colt?"

He lit his cigarette and took a deep drag. "I don't know. I guess I'll wait and see where life leads me. I've pretty much always done it that way." He removed his hat and hung it, too, around the saddle horn by its string. He ran a hand through his long dark hair, then turned to tie his shirt into his gear, the cigarette still in his mouth. "How about you? Why are you doing this, Sunny? You should be back in Chicago, making plans for a grand wedding, not out here riding like a wild woman who's scared to death of her future."

Sunny looked away, wondering if he knew what seeing him bare-chested did to her—his dark skin glistening in the sun, that cigarette between those full lips, those gentle hazel eyes. He was raw power, so sure, so handsome, so forbidden. "Who said I was scared?"

"Nobody. It's just written all over your face, that's all. Does it have something to do with marrying Blaine? You think you're going to find some kind of answer out here?"

She shook out her own hair, enjoying the feel of letting the long blond tresses fall free. "I don't know. I've never been sure about Blaine, and yet I should be." She sighed deeply. "I should be the happiest woman in the world right now. I have everything . . . everything." Her voice trailed off.

"That depends on what *everything* means. Look at what you have compared to me, and I pretty much feel *I* have everything, yet you could buy and sell me a million times over."

She stared off at the higher bluffs on the horizon. "No, Colt. No one buys and sells someone like you. You're your own man. You aren't impressed by money, and you don't judge people by it. That's why I feel so good when I'm with you, in spite of how hard it is for us to be just friends. With you I don't have to put on any airs, pretend I'm something I'm not."

"Do you pretend around Blaine?"

"Sometimes." She met his eyes. "I'm sorry. I know this is hard for you, and that I promised to let you go on with your life and me with mine. I know it's best we have absolutely nothing to do with each other, but when I think of never seeing you again, or even being able to write you, or—" She looked at him pleadingly, her eyes tearing. "Once I marry Blaine, it really will have to end. That's why I had to come out here, Colt. It isn't fair to you, and it makes no sense at all; but I felt almost led out here against my better judgment." She reached back and took a deep breath. "Now I don't regret it at all. This has been the most wonderful day I can remember since when Father and I came out here and he let me ride with you. It's strange, isn't it, how people move in and out of each other's lives—how some things change so much but other things stay the same, like the land. When I come out here it's as though the last ten years never happened. "

Colt smoked quietly for a moment. "But they *did* happen, Sunny. I lost my best friend, a wife, and a son; you lost your pa and became one of the most powerful women in this country. I've been through a war and a hell worse than death in that prison camp while you became part owner of a transcontinental railroad and built another grand home and offices in Omaha—became engaged to a man whose wealth probably matches or tops your own. My life has been one of tragedy and pain and dirt and sort of going on from one pointless thing to another. Yours is filled with balls and boardrooms and diamonds and soon a wedding that will make the papers in other countries. Things *do* change, people grow apart, especially those who have no business being involved in each other's lives."

She fought the tears, realizing what he was telling her. He could not be a part of her life. It was like that night at Fort Laramie, a gentle good-bye, a painful lesson in what was right and wrong. But she also remembered Vi's words about following her heart, about how love could conquer great obstacles. Did Colt believe that? She sniffed and wiped her tears, refusing to look at him.

"Dammit, Sunny, don't cry. I told you that ten years ago." He took another long drag on the cigarette, suddenly feeling awkward. He had spoiled her happy day. *Damn her!* he thought. How many times had he said that to himself? God, he loved her, and that was the hell of it. Should he tell her? How could it possibly help anything? It would only make everything worse.

She straightened in her saddle, retying her canteen. "I'll always treasure our friendship, Colt. One thing no one can take from me is my memories, or my dreams." She held her chin higher and faced him. "I'll race you," she told him.

"What?"

She gave him a daring look, a new boldness in her eyes. "I said I'll race you. If you catch me and manage to pull me off my horse, you've won!" She charged away, and Colt sat there a minute, wondering what she was up to. What was this sudden change in conversation? She was like a crazy woman today, and she had turned his feelings a thousand different ways.

He watched her, the way her bottom fit her saddle, the way her hair blew in the wind. Her daring look stirred his pride, and the race was on. He kicked Dancer into a hard run, manly desires stirring in him at the challenge of catching her. He held the reins with one hand and smashed out his cigarette against his saddle horn with the other, tossing the stub aside, and leaning into the ride. "Get up there, Dancer," he shouted to the horse.

Dancer's mane flew up into Colt's face as he galloped up and down more sandhills. He noticed Sunny veer to the west rather than north, and he turned Dancer, taking a cut between two more sandhills and emerging near Sunny as she came around the end of one hill. She screamed and laughed when she saw him, and now he knew he could catch her.

He came closer, the determination to reach her now a burning need. It went against all reason, was totally foreign to all sense of maturity. They were like children for the moment, and yet not children at all. The emotions it stirred in him to think of catching her were dangerous, yet he could not stop himself. He came ever closer, and now he was on her!

Sunny screamed when she felt his strong arm come around her. Suddenly, she was free of her horse and sitting sideways on Dancer, a powerful arm holding her. She covered her face and laughed as Colt slowed his horse. "Now you are my captive," he teased.

She threw her head back and faced him, and both of them

sobered. For a moment they sat there breathing heavily from the ride, watching each other.

"We had better go catch your horse," he finally told her.

"We'll find it later," she answered. She moved her hands to touch his powerful arms, ran her fingers over his bare shoulders. "Tell me, Colt. What does an Indian do with his captive?"

For a moment everything went silent for him. Nothing existed but the utterly beautiful woman in his arms, her tempting mouth, her open blouse, her blue eyes, her golden hair. He moved a hand to rest against the flat of her belly. "He takes her to his tipi and makes her his slave," he answered, his voice gruff with passion.

She touched his face. "That's what I want you to do with me, Colt. Make me your slave—today, tonight, tomorrow."

He shook his head. "Sunny—"

She touched his lips. "Don't say it, Colt." Her eyes glistened with tears. "I don't know what's right and wrong anymore, and today I don't care. I just want you. I've always wanted you." A tear slipped down her cheek. "It can't be anybody else, Colt, not the first time. I—"

His kiss cut off her words, a deep, hot kiss that removed any remaining inhibitions. She could barely get her breath for the thrill of it, the ecstasy of his hand moving to her breast, the ache of womanly desires that surged in her when his tongue moved between her lips. Dancer moved slightly, and she clung to Colt. He left her lips for a moment, keeping one arm around her as he slid off the horse and pulled her after him.

From then on they were each so possessed with passion and need that nothing else existed for them. He pulled her into the grass, and they both felt consumed by need and long-repressed desires. His kisses were hard and deep, leaving her no time to reason or to object, and hardly able to get her breath. She suspected that even if she wanted to stop him, she surely could not now. And why would she want to? This was what she had wanted for so long, what she had dreamed about for years; but it was so much more exciting and glorious than she imagined.

# INTIMATE STRANGERS
by
Alexandra Thorne
author of DESERT HEAT

*At thirty-two Jade Howard was facing a world of shattered dreams: once a bestselling novelist with all of Hollywood at her feet, she was now the critics' favorite target. And all she wanted was to get away. . . .*

*But they say you should beware of what you wish for, for in a picturesque hotel in Santa Fe, Jade will slip into a flame-colored dress—and wake up in another woman's life, with another woman's friends, her home . . . and her husband.*

*He is an intimate stranger, tall, dark, devastating—and hell-bent on driving his wife to adultery and divorce. It almost works . . . until Duncan Carlisle falls in love again, with the ravishing interloper he thinks is his wife. How can Jade tell him that the lady in his bed and in his heart is not who she seems? It is a risk she must take, and soon . . . before the real Megan Carlisle returns . . . before time itself tries to wrench two lovers apart.*

Duncan had been riding for an hour, thinking about his lunch with Megan. He had enjoyed being with her, talking to her, listening to her, looking at her. Had a stranger walked in, he would have been convinced they were a happily married couple. God knows, Megan was trying. Could he believe what she said about wanting to start over?

She had seemed sincere.

After ten years of marriage, he thought he knew every nuance of her voice. He could usually tell when she was lying, and this time he could swear she had been telling the truth. She wanted a second chance to make their marriage work. To be perfectly honest, if she continued to act the way she had the last few days, so did he.

He reined his horse to a stop. "What do you think, Excalibur?" he asked the Arabian stallion. "Should I give Megan another chance?"

Why not? he answered himself. What did he have to lose? He turned Excalibur back toward Rancho Cielo and spurred the horse to a gallop. Half an hour later, he rode into the stable, jumped off the horse's back, unsaddled him, and although he felt guilty about putting the horse up wet, led the stallion into his stall.

Megan wasn't in the kitchen when he walked in, although she had obviously washed their lunch dishes before leaving. He expected to find her in their bedroom, but she wasn't there either. Walking back toward the living room, he heard sounds coming from the den.

Megan was seated at his desk, going through his papers. Stock certificates, canceled checks, insurance policies, and his personal correspondence lay scattered in front of her. The hopeful feeling that had swelled within him on the ride home dissolved. Anger replaced it.

"What the hell are you doing?" he asked, walking up behind her and pulling her from the chair.

The papers in her hands spilled to the floor as he spun her around to face him.

"I was just . . ."

"Just what? Trying to figure how much money you'd get if I didn't change my mind about the divorce?"

She tried to pull away but he held her fast. She had been so disarmingly sweet an hour ago. Now he realized it had just been a ruse. The bitch. She had betrayed his trust again. Rage surged in his chest as he glared down at her.

Jade wanted to look away from the fire burning in Duncan's eyes, but his fury riveted her. She didn't dare tell him why she had been snooping through his papers, yet her continued silence seemed to heighten his wrath.

Her breath caught in her throat, her pulse pounded in her ears as he gripped her harder. She could feel the heat pounding from his body, the same heat that had been so comforting in bed last night. Now she took no solace from that warmth. She feared it, feared what it was making her feel.

Duncan was magnificent in his anger. Compelling. She knew she ought to struggle, try to free herself. But her body had stopped responding to her mind. She continued to stare into his eyes, seeing pain there—and something else. Desire. God. Her stomach tightened as she realized that he wanted her.

Her arms seemed to rise of their own volition. Her fingers tangled in his hair as she pulled his head down to hers. A wildness burst into life inside her. She heard him groan, a primal sound that sent urgent messages coursing through her blood. Then her lips met his.

Duncan pulled her against him and kissed her so hard, he knew her lips would be bruised. She had used sex as a weapon before. How like her to use it now.

He wanted to punish her, to hurt her the way she had just hurt him. Instead he found himself drowning in the sweet curves that fit his body so perfectly. Her lips parted under the pressure of his kiss, and he explored her mouth with his tongue while his eager hands explored her body with rough urgency. He gripped her buttocks, forcing the swell of her stomach against him.

She was so hot. He wanted to bury himself inside her, to devour every inch of her flesh—the ruby-tipped breasts, the deep well of her navel, the generous black bush that hid the honeyed depths of her.

Her tongue found his, flaring his lust so that it burned even brighter than his anger. He felt her nipples harden through the cloth of his shirt and remembered the sweet ache of sucking them. She met his rising passion with a frenzied need of her own that implored, urged, taunted. Megan. Oh God. *Megan.*

Suddenly, without even realizing he was going to do it, he pushed her away. He wanted her, dammit, with a hunger that blasted his bones. But he'd see himself in hell before he made love to her again. An hour of pleasure wasn't worth a lifetime of misery and regret.

Jade was so weak with desire, she wasn't sure she could stand without Duncan's arms around her. She clenched her hands and locked her knees to keep from swaying, then opened her eyes wide to gaze at the man she wanted more than she had ever wanted anything or anyone. She ached to give herself to him, to yield up the secrets of her body and her soul.

Now she saw rejection plainly written on his face. She had seen that look on a man's face before, the day Paul broke their engagement. Seeing it again made her want to weep, to scream out her anguish. She wanted to fly at Duncan and rake her nails across his face, to draw blood to match the hemorrhaging wounds he'd inflicted on her soul.

But she wouldn't give him the satisfaction. Instead, she stiffened her spine and walked out of the den without a backward glance. She would have liked to keep right on walking straight out of the house, up the drive, out of Duncan Carlisle's life. But she didn't have that option.

She had never been more aroused by a man. The realization that he didn't want her, could barely stand to touch her, made her sick. Where were her pride and independence now? Trampled under his feet, that's where. Although she had never been much of a drinker, she would have gladly gotten blind drunk. She didn't have that option either.

It took all her courage, all her considerable willpower to force herself to do what she had to do. She returned to the quiet of the master bedroom and, with a calculation born of desperation, began cataloguing what she'd learned so far.

Duncan Carlisle was successful, wealthy, a gifted artist who would go down in history as the finest painter of his era. In addition he was handsome, and she now knew that, despite the coldness he often displayed with her, he was a passionate lover when he wanted to be. But she would see him in hell before she let him touch her again.

The only thing she knew about Megan was that she had a passion for clothes. It wasn't enough—not by a damn sight. Jade sat down at Megan's dressing table and looked at herself in the mirror, comparing her reflection to the woman in the photographs.

She saw the differences so clearly. Why didn't Duncan? And what had happened to Megan? Had she too passed through the door to time? Was Aurora the key? Was it the dress? Or was it some unforeseen combination of circumstances that might never happen again?

She knew nothing about time-travel theories, except that it was a popular topic in science-fiction novels. Perhaps serious books had been written about the possibility, though. Perhaps in the Sante Fe library . . . No. She rejected the idea. From what she recalled, Einstein had just developed his space-time theory. A local library wasn't going to be any help.

Her shoulders sagged. She sighed heavily. She was stuck here, trapped in another woman's life, sleeping with her husband. And she had to face it. Part of her wanted to stay.

She opened the top drawer of the dressing table. Megan's cosmetics filled it, and she began applying them, as if she could absorb the other woman's personality through her pores. When she finished, she studied herself in the mirror again. That was better. The makeup did make her look more like Megan. But what good would that do unless she could think and act like her as well?

She simply had no choice. She would have to tell Duncan the truth tonight. Grimacing at the possible consequences, she idly opened the bottom drawer where Megan kept her jewels. Dazzled by the array, she picked up the velvet-lined tray and put it on her lap. She was about to shut the drawer when she realized the tray had covered a series of slender leather-bound books. Bending down for a closer look, she saw each one was stamped with a year, beginning with 1919 and ending with 1929. They had to be Megan's diaries.

Bingo, she exulted, and picked up the first volume.

# LIGHTNING
by Patricia Potter
author of
LAWLESS and RAINBOW

LIGHTNING *is a lush, dramatic, and truly emotional historical romance, set during the Civil War. Lauren Bradley was the new coquette in the tropical port of Nassau. Only the kindly shopkeeper knew the beautiful young woman had agreed to avenge her brother's death by becoming a Yankee spy in this stronghold of Confederate blockade runners.*

*Englishman Adrian Cabot was the most daring of those who ran supplies to the South. As handsome as sin and fearless as the devil, he had sworn to recover his family's honor with the profits from his dangerous missions. No one knew of the need that burned within him—except Lauren, who heard in his bold laughter the sound of a wounded soul.*

*Their meeting was fated. She was sent by Washington to sabotage his ship. He was sent by destiny to steal her heart. Together on board the* Specter, *they were swept into passion's treacherous sea, tasting deeply of ecstasy and the danger of war.*

*In the following scene, Lauren and Adrian are aboard the* Specter, *the engines of which she plans to sabotage. Her discovery that Adrian has made a wager with another captain over who would first win her affection steels her resolve to stop his blockade-running. . . .*

"Lauren." Adrian's voice was soft in her ear, and she returned to the moment, to the seductive night, and the danger. His danger. Her own danger when she was with him. Dear God, how could she survive this?

Hate him, she urged herself. Hate him for what he is, for what he's doing, for what he wagered.

But that was like hating the warm, bright sun, hating the brightness while the body drank up the warmth.

"Frightened?" he said, his hand on her shoulder tightening ever so slightly.

Lauren kept her gaze away from him. She couldn't look at him now, at the eyes so deep a blue she could never find its source, or identify the currents that ran in them. She didn't understand him, or the many contradictions she saw in him.

"Yes," she said. But not for the reason he believed.

"The run is really fairly safe," he said, leaning over, his words a soft whisper in the night as his breath touched her ear, and she shivered.

His hand dropped from her shoulder, and both of his arms went around her waist. She found herself leaning back against him. It was so natural, as if it was meant to be, this fusing of bodies.

The lamps on the ship were quenched, one by one, and she turned, looking askance at him in a night now lit only by a host of stars that were bright in the sky but flashed precious little light to the earth.

"It's time," he whispered, "to get lost in the night."

Lauren watched as distant lights also disappeared, one by one, and she and Adrian seemed alone in the total blackness of night. Even the loud voices of the crew had quieted to whispers, and only the sound of water against the hull made music in the vast emptiness.

The sudden void matched the hollowness inside her. Adrian's arms were still around her, and something deep inside her relished the comfort of his embrace. But it was all false, she reminded herself. He doesn't mean it, any more than she did.

She forced some words out. "Isn't it dangerous . . . without lights?"

"Johnny's the best pilot in the business. He can sense—see—every reef, every jut of land in the blackest of nights. Damned if I know how. Part owl, I suppose."

*Keep talking. Keep talking so you won't feel.* Lauren shifted slightly, and Adrian's arms moved with her. The friction of skin against skin, body against body, sent waves of painful pleasure washing over her. She wanted his hands to move again, to reexperience those wonderful sensations that made her feel so alive.

There was a tug on her skirt, and she looked down, barely able to see Socrates in the darkness. Then she tipped her head upward. The shadow of Adrian's head, the outline of those hard, clean features so close, came even closer as she felt his lips touch her cheek and his hands turn her ever so slightly so she was at his side rather than in front of him.

Her heart thumped so loudly she thought he must hear. Her hand trembled when it lay on the railing. His lips moved to touch her lips, softly, searchingly.

Lauren knew they were lost in the shadow, in the inky darkness, so the members of the crew could not see. It was as if they were alone in an infinite empty vault, nothing real except each other. She felt his lips press tighter against her mouth, and she realized she was responding, her mouth opening to his gentle probing.

Emotions flooded her. Wild, runaway emotions. Pleasure. Need. Anticipation. The danger, the tension, made everything so much more intense, magnified her sensations until she didn't know how she could bear them, to hold them inside without exploding. She was learning quickly what Adrian had meant about danger.

Or was it the danger?

She stepped back frantically. "No," she whispered, and his arms loosened from around her. His lips whispered against her cheek, and then his hand caught her chin, making her look up at him. She couldn't see his features well, but in her mind she saw his slight smile, the question in his eyes.

"You're like quicksilver, Miss Bradley," he said softly. "You keep running away from me. Why?"

*Because I hate you. And I'm so afraid I also love you.*

"I'm tired," she said aloud, her voice unsteady.

Adrian sighed. His head started to lower again, and Lauren knew he meant to kiss her, to kiss away her rejection, but she spun away, afraid that he would do just that.

"Please, Adrian."

"We'll talk tomorrow," he said, his voice suddenly hard and uncompromising, and she knew she was going to need to give some explanations the next day. She knew he must be totally confused, the way she yielded one moment and ran the next. The good Lord knew she was confused!

"I'll walk you to the cabin," he said, his hands leaving her as he stooped down and swept up Socrates. Adrian's right hand took her arm firmly, guiding her through the dark night air to the steps that led down to the cabin. The interior was even darker than the deck, and she wondered how he stepped so surely. She felt totally blind, completely at his mercy.

The engines hummed as Adrian's hand steadied her uncertain steps, his warmth and scent intoxicating in the cocoon of the ship, of the night. She stumbled, and his arm went around her again, keeping her from falling. Lauren felt as if he were an integral part of her, and she knew she would never be whole again when he was gone.

*When he was gone!*

And then they were at the cabin, and he'd opened the door. He released her, and she heard the sound of a match striking, and the flare of a lantern. "It's safe to use a light in here," he said. "There are no windows."

The lantern, really a strange-looking oil lamp designed specifically for ships, was hung from a hook, its flickering flame sending darts of light around the cabin, illuminating his face. There were so many questions in his expression—questions she could never answer.

Socrates jumped to the floor and went over to his bed.

"I'll take him with me," Adrian said.

"Why don't you leave him here?"

"Are you quite sure about that?" Adrian's voice was now tinged with amusement. "Sometimes he decides he prefers the bed. You might wake up with a bony paw clutching at you."

"At least he'll be company."

His eyes sparkled, the deep blue of them catching fire from the flame. "I find myself jealous. And of a monkey. I'll have no pride left, Miss Bradley," he teased.

"I think that unlikely," she retorted.

"You do unprecedented damage to it."

"I believe you will recover."

"Doubtful." An endearingly wistful smile played over his face. Another ploy? "Good night, Captain."

"Adrian," he insisted.

"Lord Adrian," she said, trying to keep a certain distance.

"Lord Ridgely to be correct," he said dryly. "You sound as if you dislike lords?"

"I've heard they play games," she charged unwisely.

"What kind of games?"

"With hearts." *With my heart*.

He was silent, his eyes dark and secretive, a muscle twitching in his cheek. She wished she knew why.

"Don't they?"

"Not all of them. Do all women play games?" There was a sudden harsh edge to his voice.

Drat the man. He had a way of putting her on the defensive. Of turning her words against her. And he had wagered on her! Her anger rose again, protecting her from her own weakness. But she knew she had to guard against that too. She had already said too much. But the skin where he'd touched her still tingled, still burned, and she knew if he kissed her, she would be lost again.

She prayed briefly, and her prayers were answered. His voice low, rumbling through her consciousness, made her reply unnecessary.

"I have to get up on deck. These waters are still dangerous. Good night . . . Lauren."

There was an unusual curtness to his words, and she felt a now-familiar pain stab through her. If his censure hurt now, dear God, how much was it going to hurt when he learned the truth?